KAIJU WARS

ERIC S. BROWN

SEVERED PRESS
HOBART TASMANIA

KAIJU WARS

Copyright © 2017 Eric S. Brown
Copyright © 2017 by Severed Press

WWW.SEVEREDPRESS.COM

ISBN: 978-1-925597-93-6

KAIJU WARS

The Motta pulsed with power. Its tendrils stretched out, throbbing as electrical surges ran them in place of the wires that would have normally powered an Old World vehicle like this one. One of the tendrils was loose though. Very carefully, with his gloved hand, Sergeant Watson reached down and lifted the tendril back into place. Slamming the hood of the jeep, Sergeant Watson straightened up to his full, towering, six-foot-nine height.

"Like I thought. It was just a loose connection, boys," he told Privates McMillian and Joster. "She shouldn't be giving you any more issues now."

"Thank you, sir," McMillian barked.

Joster had already slid into the jeep's driver seat and was cranking it up. Sergeant Watson was glad for it. Time was not on their side and the jeep was blocking the path of the rest of the convoy. It had broken down in the middle of the road right in front of his command car. Sergeant Watson was used to that kind of luck after five years in the Greenery's defense force. If something was going to breakdown or go wrong, it always seemed to happen at the worst time and in the worst possible way. He knew he could have left McMillian and Joster. Their jeep wasn't exactly an essential part of the convoy. The other vehicles could easily have driven a bit off the road to get around their broken-down jeep, but he was a firm believer in not leaving anyone behind. Word was that the Techs were on the move in the area and making a push towards the Greenery's outer-lying towns. If the rumors about the Tech forces were true, leaving them could very well have been a death sentence for the two men. As it stood, the entire convoy would be little more than a moving target if they encountered the Techs. When they had left Blossom Range, the Techs were still being held back at Pickman's Point. Though the run of Bio-matter was important to the cause, there simply hadn't been the manpower or firepower to equip the convoy as a truly combat-ready force since the danger to it had appeared minimal at the time.

Sergeant Watson slapped the hood of the jeep, indicating for Joster to kick it into gear as soon as he had cleared it front, and headed for his command car. Corporal Hanson was waiting on him there, a frown still deeply cutting into the features of his face.

"Oh let it go, Hanson," Sergeant Watson told him. "You know me fixing that jeep myself was the fastest way to get it moving again."

Hanson opened the rear passenger door of the command car for him as Sergeant Watson approached it. From the treatment Hanson gave him, one would think that he was a fragging general or something instead of a mere sergeant. Private First Class Michael Hanson though was the most by-the-book trooper Sergeant Watson had ever encountered. While he couldn't fault Hanson for it, sometimes it really grated on his nerves. Hanson closed the door after him as he got into the command car and walked around to get into it on the other side. The command car's driver got it moving quickly, following Joster's jeep ahead of them.

In the Old World, the command car Sergeant Watson rode in was once some kind of luxury vehicle, a limo he thought it was called. It had been refit with a Greenery power source and its body heavily armored up. Above where he and Private Hanson sat was a sliding opening in its ceiling that allowed them access to the machine gun mounted on its roof.

Following along behind their command car and Joster's patrol jeep were three heavy transport trucks and two, Greenery-made, combat cars. Though the command car and all of the jeeps had machine gun emplacements, the combat cars were sporting the only true firepower the convoy had its disposal. They were outfitted with Mech Killer missile tubes. Each combat car carried two such tubes, each loaded with a single shot. It wasn't much but it was all they had should the dung hit the fan.

The Greenery and the Techs had been a war for over twenty years now ever since they had discovered each other's existence. Sergeant Watson's father had died in Battle Jawall some ten years ago. His death was the reason Sergeant Watson had signed up for service in the Greenery's defense force. All he had ever wanted since he had put his father's empty coffin in the ground, as there hadn't been enough of him left to ship home from the front, was to kill as many Techs as he could. And for a while, he had done just that until a promotion had earned him a post at the small bio-center of Blossom Range. For the last year or so, he had been regulated to running convoys like this one from the bio-center back to the Greenery's fortress of a capital city.

Most of those under his command were either merely boys or had something off about them which kept them from being deployed to the front. It wasn't that the Greenery was losing the war. In fact, when it really came down it, they were winning it, but the bulk of the defense force was always held back to defend the capital city. It was the heart of the Greenery, where the truly massive bio-centers spawned not only the power sources that ran its civilization but also where the great Kaiju were manufactured. Those massive monsters were the key to ending the war once and for all, and everyone in the Greenery knew it from the highest powers to the commonest civilian.

Sergeant Watson was rocked about in his seat as the ground the command car drove along shook beneath it. His heart skipped a beat inside his chest as his eyes went wide with fear. He'd felt such shaking of the ground enough times over his years in the service to know exactly what had caused it.

"Incoming Mech!" Private Joster cried out over the unit's Psi-link.

Sergeant Watson tapped into the unit's psi-link using his command abilities to see through the eyes of his men. He couldn't see the mech that Joster had warned the convoy about but he did see two hover tanks. They came, gliding over the sands, on a direct route for the convoy. Their main guns opened up, booming like thunder. One round impacted the road between the command car and Joster's jeep. His driver had swerved at just the right moment to avoid the round blowing the car to flaming bits. Even so, the round flung chunks of the road at the command car like shrapnel from a detonating grenade. They hammered at its armor. One thudded off the side of the car beside where Sergeant Watson sat within it. He flinched at the noise, throwing himself sideways in the seat. Others struck the car's roof, hood, and forward window. He could hear the driver upfront cursing as the car jerked again as this time it swung in the opposite direction to avoid the pit the exploding round had dug in the road.

The second incoming round made contact with one of the heavy transport trucks. The truck buckled upwards from the impact and then finished ripping apart as the round fully detonated. In little more than seconds, there was nothing left of the truck other than scattered pieces of burning debris that littered the road where the heavy vehicle had been roaring along at its maximum speed.

"Return fire!" Sergeant Watson ordered through the psi-link but his men were already getting into position to do just that. Screw-ups some of them might be but none of them were stupid enough not to put a fight when faced with what was otherwise certain death.

The other two trucks in the convoy had stopped and their crews were diving out of them to engage the tanks. Sergeant Watson could see two men from one of the trucks readying a Swarm launcher as the convoy's two combat cars veered onto an intercept course towards the approaching hover tanks. The lead combat car's right side tube fired, sending a mech-killer missile howling through the air at the closer of the two hover tanks. A startled grunt escaped Sergeant Watson as he saw the missile actually hit the tank. He had expected the tank to dodge the missile given the speed the tank was traveling at but luck appeared to have taken his side for once. The mech-killer missile tore through the tank's thick, forward armor and then detonated within in the tank itself. The tank burst apart like an overripe melon being smashed by a sledgehammer. Burning pieces of the tank were flung skyward to rain back down onto the sands.

The convoy's other combat car never had the chance to fire at the second tank. The second tank's driver had put the pedal down, pouring on even more speed, and closed on it as the tank's gunner behind the topside-mounted machine gun cut the jeep and those within it to shreds. The jeep, its driver dead at the wheel, veered off the road and crashed into one of the large rocks that were scattered about the valley. Its front end folded up against the rock until its metal couldn't give anymore and the jeep bounced backwards to sit, dead and broken, on the sand beside the road.

The two men with the Swarm launcher had it ready now. Sergeant Watson touched their minds through the psi-link and knew they were taking aim at the remaining tank. The tank had changed its course and was on a direct route for the two surviving heavy transport trucks. Its main gun flashed reducing one of them to exploding shards of metal and burnt geysers of bio-gel.

There was a thunking sound as the two men fired the Swarm launcher. The beehive-shaped bomb it spat shattered as it struck the side of the enemy tank, releasing the millions of nearly microscopic insects it contained. They ate away at the tank's armor at a speed that still seemed impossible to Sergeant Watson despite the many times he had seen the tiny Swarmers used on mechs and tanks before. It was as if the tank's side evaporated in an instant, exposing the men inside it. The tank wobbled as the Swarmers ate away part of the underside fans that kept it moving and above the sand it glided over. It veered away from the convoy, trying to make a run for it, but barely made it fifty yards before the Swarmers must have gnawed on something volatile, maybe its fusion core. The explosion was the largest so far in the battle and sent shockwaves of force out that battered Sergeant

Watson's command car and knocked the exposed troopers who had abandoned their trucks to fight from their feet.

The intensity of Joster's panic drew Sergeant Watson's attention back to him through the psi-link. His mind touched Joster's just as the private hurled himself from the driver's seat of his jeep. Joster thudded onto the road, rolling out of the path of the giant metal foot that came down on the jeep crushing it and Private McMillian beneath its weight. Through Joster's eyes, Sergeant Watson looked up in horror at the mech that charged onto the road in front of the stopped convoy.

The metal of the mech's armor gleamed in the sunlight. The mech stood at least fifty feet tall, towering over Joster where the private lay. Sergeant Watson recognized it as a single pilot, Ferret class, designed for maximum speed and maneuverability. It carried a belt fed gigantic weapon in its hands and lifted it to aim at the last of the convoy's heavy transport trucks. The gun chattered, its sound like one sonic boom after another as the rounds it fired pounded the transport truck, ripping the vehicle to shreds where it sat.

The driver of Sergeant Watson's command car had continued to take it on a course away from the combat. Though it was out of the battle proper, it was still in range of the mech's weapon. With one of the convoy's combat cars and the transport trucks that made up its heart destroyed, there was no reason to stick around and continue the engagement with the mech.

"All units, disengage! Break south and get the frag out of the thing's range of fire!" Sergeant Watson screamed with his mind over the unit's psi-link. Doing so would leave the handful of men from the truck crews at the Tech's mercy but there was nothing he could do about that.

The two men with the Swarm launcher were busy reloading the weapon as the two jeeps broke off their course for the enemy mech and swerved wide into a turn that would bring them about and away from it. Even as they did so, their gunners continued firing the mounted machine guns of the two jeeps at the mech. High-velocity rounds sparked and pinged off the armor of the mech's body, accomplishing little more than scratching its paint.

The Mech ignored the two jeeps. Its attention was focused entirely on the convoy's remaining combat car that was charging towards it. The combat car's left side tube fired. A mech-killer missile streaked outward from it towards the Ferret-class mech. For all its speed, the missile never reached its target. The Ferret's pilot deployed countermeasures, a series of flare-like projectiles bursting from the twin launchers that rose up on its shoulders sprayed the air, creating a wall of flame in front of it. It was impossible to tell how many of them struck the missile but they got their job done. It exploded several yards out from the mech. The explosion rocked the Ferret-class mech where it stood, pushing the hulking metal monster back, but its pilot managed to keep it on its feet. The combat car tried to veer away as the mech raised its massive gun at the vehicle and squeezed the weapon's trigger. Its first burst nearly cut the combat car in two, knocking it out of the air. The combat car thudded to the ground, skidding along, carried forward by its own momentum, until it must have hit something under the sand that sent it flying end of over end to land in a fiery flash of flame and exploding shrapnel. The mech fired a second burst of rounds into the blazing wreckage of the combat car, scooting its remains along in the sand from the power and force of their impact.

With the combat car taken out, the mech turned its attention to the fleeing jeeps and Sergeant Watson's command car. The command car was already almost out of the mech's range of fire but the two jeeps were still close enough to be easy targets. The mech's massive gun roared again, sending a stream of fire at the slower of the two jeeps. They ripped away the jeep's rear wheels and its back section. Had the jeep been a tech vehicle, it would surely have gone up in flames from its gas tank being ignited. It ran on the bio-power of that was the Greenery's trademark, however, so instead of exploding, it careened sideways, its front two wheels continuing to try to pull it forward. Sergeant Watson had felt the two men in the jeep die as the rounds from the mech's gun had reduced them to red pulp that smeared the inside of what was left of the jeep.

Then it was all over as quickly as it had begun. The command car and the last jeep drove around the base of a small hill to the south that blocked the mech's line of fire. The Ferret-class mechs were built for close in combat anyway so they were out of the range of its weapon but the added deterrent of the small hill as cover meant they had escaped with their lives unless the mech's pilot opted to hunt them down. Sergeant Watson figured that was highly unlikely. The mech's mission had to be to stop the transport of the bio-gel and it had already achieved that goal.

"Take us home," Sergeant Watson ordered the command car's driver and slumped deeper into his seat. Private Hanson, who shared the back of the command car with him, was frowning.

"That was too close for comfort, sir," Hanson said, using the backside of his hand to wipe at the sweat that covered his brow beneath his short chopped, brown hair. He had taken his helmet off and placed it on the seat next to him.

"Tell me about it," Sergeant Watson grumbled.

****

Joster covered his ears as he ran, his legs pumping beneath him. The booming of the Ferret-class mech's massive weapon still almost blew out his eardrums. The two hover tanks and the mech appeared to be the only Tech forces in the immediate area. If there were more, surely they would have moved forward by now.

The convoy's command car with Sergeant Watson inside it and the last of the jeeps had disappeared from sight and the mech's attention had turned to the soldiers of the convoy's truck crews on the road. There were five of them in all, four men and one woman. Two of the men were aiming a Swarm launcher at the mech as the hulking, metal monster brought its gun around in their direction.

The Swarm launcher spat its beehive-shaped round at the mech before it could bring its gun to bear on them. For a moment, Joster thought the two men might have actually gotten lucky enough to bring the mech down, but the mech threw itself to the side with an almost human agility, dodging their shot. As it regained its balance from the hurried maneuver, the Greenery soldiers on the road scattered, running in different directions. The tactic didn't help them at all. The mech simply hosed the entire section of the road with a continuous stream of automatic fire. The soldiers splattered apart like squashed bugs as the mech's rounds cut them down. Their lives had bought him time though. Joster dove behind a large boulder and took cover there. He didn't dare sneak a glance around the rock to see what the mech was doing. He knew most mechs carried rather impressive sonar suites, but he still prayed the mech's pilot wouldn't bother looking for other survivors unless it was threatened.

Not even daring to breathe except when he couldn't hold his breath any longer, and even then doing so as quietly as he could, he waited for the mech to make the next move. The only weapon he carried was his sidearm. His rifle had been in the jeep when he had flung himself out of it and crushed along with his friend, McMillian, when the mech's foot had come down on its center.

For long moments, there was no sound at all then finally Joster had the mech's servos kicked into gear. He listened to the mech's heavy footfalls as it darted for the far end of the valley back towards the way it had come from. Even after those footfalls had faded to silence, he waited another solid ten minutes before emerging from behind the boulder he had taken cover behind.

Wreckage and debris were everywhere along the road and strewn about other random parts of the valley's sand as well. As far as he could tell, he was the only living soul that remained in the valley. Joster tried to tap into his unit's psi-link but there was nothing left that his mind could reach. Sergeant Watson and the surviving members of his unit had to be out of range of his weak attempt. Joster had never been very psionically gifted but it had been worth the effort to try. At least he knew now that he really was alone.

The midday sun was hot and cruel without the air-conditioning of his jeep. It blazed down on him, as he stood there trying to figure out what to do. He knew he needed to get moving. The mech could return at any moment with more Techs accompanying it. Staying where he was put him at risk of being captured or worse if the mech returned or other Tech units entered the valley.

He desperately needed water and supplies though, and the only place he might find them was among the wreckage of the convoy and the remains of the two Tech hover tanks. Joster sighed, shaking his head, and started towards the blood-smeared forward section of the jeep the mech had shot as it tried to flee. Most of the other vehicles were burning.

It took several minutes for Joster to finish the grizzly task of digging through what was left of the jeep. When he was done, his hands were covered in the blood of its crew, but he had found a canteen and a Swarm grenade. He used part of the water and strip of cloth he tore from his uniform to clean them before fastening them both his belt. The grenade dangled on his left hip and the water beside it. He didn't want to position either near his sidearm so they wouldn't get in the way if he needed to draw it quickly.

The canteen was only three-fourths full. That amount of water wouldn't last long out here so he was going to have to ration it carefully. Joster knew he should continue looking for more supplies but after the horror of searching through what was left of the jeep, he couldn't bring himself to do it. Instead, he set out walking in the direction Sergeant Watson's command car had disappeared in. He kept his pace slow and steady so as not to push his body too hard in the heat, but to be truthful, it was the best he could manage anyway. The battle had taken a lot out of him, both physically and emotionally.

Joster was still walking when the sun began to sink behind the distant hills to the south.

****

Colonel Jaeger sat at his desk, scrolling through the latest batch of reports from the front lines. The war between the Greenery and Steel Heart had been raging for twenty years now, give or take a few months. During that time, both sides had their moments of glory but neither had ever achieved a decisive victory over the other and so the war continued on. He had been granted overall command of Steel Heart's forces two months ago. It wasn't something he had sought or even wanted, but with the death of his predecessor, Colonel Drake, during the last major kaiju attack on the capital, the Council of Engineers had appointed him to the task. With the kaiju pushed back and the Greenery's forces depleted from the attack on Steel Heart, Colonel Jaeger's first move was to launch an all-out offensive against the Greenery's capital. So far, things were going as he had hoped, but there were hints buried among the reports from the front that that may be changing.

Six of Steel Hearts primary mechs were deployed and advancing towards the Greenery's capital, leaving only two behind to act as a defense force should the city come under attack again. Of Steel Heart's thirty-six smaller, Wolf-class mechs, two dozen of them were deployed as part of the offensive as well along with all forty-five of the remaining hover tanks. Backed up by half of Steel Heart's infantry forces, the plan was for them to break through the long-standing lines and push their way into the heart of the Greenery. The Greenery could produce their giant kaiju far faster than Steel Heart could build the larger scale mechs needed to combat them. Wolf-class mechs and hover tanks could take out the giant kaiju but not without suffering heavy losses in the process.

There were rumors that the Greenery was on the verge of developing an even faster means of breeding the giant kaiju that were their main weapons of war. If they did, it could mean the end of Steel Heart once and for all. That was a chance that Colonel Jaeger couldn't take. It was the main reason behind his new offensive and striking while the Greenery's forces were weakened instead of focusing the resources at his disposal on the production of more mechs and tanks during in what otherwise very likely would have been a lull in the war.

The Council of Engineers didn't believe the rumors that drove him but they could at least see that the Greenery was for the time being weakened and as thus backed his plan to crush them while the chance to do existed.

Already, the forces pressing into the Greenery's territory had penetrated the lines in several places and were on track for reaching the kaiju breeding facilities of its capital. Thus far, the opposition they faced had been even less than Colonel Jaeger had expected. Two of the Greenery's bio-gel production centers had been eliminated and numerous convoys of the gel on its way to the heart of the Greenery had been intercepted and destroyed. On the surface, everything appeared to be in Steel Heart's favor but the same lack of resistance that was responsible for much of his forces' success also worried him. It didn't make sense for the Greenery not to put up more of a fight, certainly not with so many of their bio-gel production centers threatened by the incursion into their territory. Other than a few flyers, they had yet to deploy any kaiju to engage his advancing forces, which made him wonder what they were holding the great beasts in reserve for.

A chime sounded from the door to his office. Colonel Jaeger sat aside his datapad and looked in its direction. "Enter," he said loudly.

The door slid open to reveal Major Steiner, his second-in-command. From the expression on the major's face, he knew whatever news the man was bringing wasn't good.

"Colonel." Major Steiner nodded at him as he entered the office. The man moved to stand at attention in front of Colonel Jaeger's desk. "I hope I am not intruding, sir."

"Not at all, Major." Colonel Jaeger gave him a polite smile. "I was just going over the reports from the front. It seems the offensive is going even better than we hoped it would, given the current state of the Greenery's forces."

"I see." Major Steiner returned his smile. "That is good news indeed."

Colonel Jaeger stared at the major. "Are you going to tell me why you're here or are you waiting on me to guess? I can't imagine this being a purely social visit."

"Sorry, sir." Major Steiner's smile became a frown. "Councilor Sheehan requests your presence at his factory. Something has come up that requires your attention ... personally or so the councilor claims."

Colonel Jaeger glanced at his watch. "Now? The battle of Canton is less than an hour from beginning."

Canton was the largest of the outlying bio-gel production centers. It was also where the bulk of the Greenery's defense forces outside of their capital were based. The battle was a key one in terms of the continued push towards the heart of the Greenery. It needed to be dealt with. Colonel Jaeger knew that if it was merely bypassed, it would leave the Greenery defense forces in the perfect position to harass his troops all the way to the capital. It was unlikely that Canton held enough forces to truly threaten his own but such continued harassment would take its toll, and he needed as much firepower available as possible when his men reached the heart of the Greenery. It had been years since any Steel Heart forces had reached the Greenery's capital and what sort of last ditch defenses awaited them there was anyone's guess.

"The councilor was insistent, sir." Major Steiner's frown grew deeper.

Colonel Jaeger sighed. He knew he could deny the councilor's request but it would burn political capital he might need very soon if Steel Heart's advance came to a grinding halt and turned into a prolonged engagement with so much of their forces deployed so far from their own capital.

"Fine," Colonel Jaeger said at last. "Prep my car. I'll meet you at in five."

"Yes, sir." Major Steiner nodded and hurried out of his office.

Colonel Jaeger took a moment before getting up from his chair. Major Leiber was in command of the detachment that would be making the assault on Canton. He had handpicked Leiber himself for the task. If anyone could handle it, other than himself, Leiber was the woman for the job. Still, he had hoped to be a part of that battle, overseeing it via comlink. Now he was going to have to settle for reading after action reports. Putting his faith in others, no matter how competent, talented, or well-trained was a hard thing for him with so much at stake. There appeared to be no other choice, however, if he wanted to keep Councilor Sheehan as a firm supporter of his push towards the Greenery capital.

Taking one last look at the disposition of the forces directly under Major Leiber's command, he grunted, hoping they would be enough, and rose from his chair.

****

War Leader Hoyt stood atop the wall surrounding the city of Canton. He stared through the vision enhancers he held to his eyes at the approaching Tech army. His stomach rolled at the sight of them. He didn't need the vision enhancers to see the four, massive mechs that were lumbering towards the city behind the two platoons of hover tanks that were leading the assault. The lack of infantry among the Tech forces spoke volumes about their intent toward the city. The Techs had no intention of taking it and holding it as their own. It was clear that merely wanted it burnt to the ground and wiped from the face of the Earth.

"Should we release the kaiju, sir?" Lieutenant Schmitz asked.

If the Greenery had any true kaiju remaining, War Leader Hoyt wasn't privy to that information. However, the city of Canton was home to two detachments of lesser such creatures. The kaiju under his command were little more than human sized. They reminded him of velociraptors. They were fast and deadly but mainly bred to engage Tech infantry, not hover tanks and true mechs. Turning the beasts loose now was risky. The hover tanks were likely to blow the bulk of the beasts to red smears on the sand before they ever reached them.

Canton also had three tank regiments, consisting of four tanks each, that it could field as well two units of combat cars, totaling twelve all equipped with side-mounted, mech-killer missiles. All of the vehicles though were Old World ones refitted with Greenery bio-tech. Alone, they were no match for the more powerful and more advanced Tech forces in route to the city.

Lieutenant Schmitz continued to stare at him awaiting an answer.

Finally, War Leader Hoyt nodded sharply. "Release the kaiju. Have them target the mechs. With luck, they will create enough of a distraction for our tanks and combat cars to at least do some damage to the enemy hover tanks."

"Yes, sir." Lieutenant Schmitz smiled and motioned to the kaiju handlers below their position on the wall.

The gates of the city of Canton opened. A snarling stream of nearly two hundred kaiju poured through them, charging towards the Steel Heart forces approaching Canton. As they did so, the city's trio of large, double-barreled cannons began firing at the two hundred and fifty feet tall mechs that composed the rear most section of the enemy's ranks. As the kaiju sprinted forward, Canton's tanks and combat cars followed them through the gates to form a firing line just outside the city.

****

Lieutenant David Campbell sat in *Ragnarok Valkyrie*'s pilot compartment. He was strapped into the giant mech's systems to the point that they actually interfaced with his own nervous system through cybernetic ports that had been surgically added to his body. He could feel and guide the giant mech's movements as if they were own and see through its external sensors as if they were his own eyes. Right now, he was watching the mass of kaiju racing towards the hover tanks that were leading the assault on Canton. His fingers twitched, wanting desperately to open up on the monsters with *Ragnarok Valkyrie*'s weapon systems. It took a great deal of willpower not to. Major Leiber's orders were very clear: the mechs were to take no part in the initial action against the city. They were allowed to defend themselves against coming fire though.

Canton's trio of cannons had begun filling the air with lethal, bomb-like projectiles aimed at his mech and the others accompanying it. They soared over the battlefield to begin their downward arcs towards their targets. *Ragnarok Valkyrie*'s automatic fire defense systems sprang to life to engage them. Shoulder-mounted launchers sprayed .50 caliber flak into their path. The bomb like projectiles blew apart as the bullets met them. Campbell allowed himself a smirk as explosions of the prematurely detonating shells reminded him of the fireworks displays he had seen as a child growing up in the capital of Steel Heart.

A random shell made it through the defensive fire of the four mechs and struck *Hulking Diablo* on its chest. It exploded there in a flash of light and heat. The impact caused *Hulking Diablo* to take a step backwards in order to keep its footing but did little other damage. The armor of the four giant mechs had been designed to go head to head with the Greenery's great kaiju. Campbell knew that even if the entire barrage of shells had struck them, *Ragnarok Valkyrie* and the others would have only taken minor damage at best.

With *Ragnarok Valkyrie*'s auto-defense systems handling the fire from the city's cannons, he turned his attention back to the battle on the ground below in front of the giant mech. The hover tanks were hammering the charging kaiju with their main guns. Barrels flashed, discharging bolts of green energy that rained death onto the monsters. Each blast killed a dozen kaiju or more where it struck their ranks but still the monsters charged onward mindlessly, lost in the animal bloodlust of their kind.

Despite the heavy losses they were taking, the fastest of the kaiju reached the hover tanks. The hover tanks were not the slow, barely maneuverable of the old world. They broke formation, speeding away from each other to better engage the monsters as their top-mounted machine guns chattered, their streams of fire splattering kaiju blood and guts over the sand.

Campbell watched as two kaiju managed to leap onto one of the tanks. The tank's topside gunner tried to bring his machine gun around at them but the action was too slow. One of the kaiju took his head from his shoulders with a single swipe of its claws. A geyser of red exploded from the stub of his mangled neck as his body slumped over to lean forward against the now-silent machine gun. The other kaiju sunk its claws into the gunner's body and effortlessly hurled it out of the turret where it lay. The tank's driver was desperately trying to shake the beasts off of it. The tank zigged and zagged wildly about as it built speed. That was when the Greenery tanks outside the city's walls joined the battle.

The hover tank with the two kaiju clinging to its topside took a round fired by one of the Greenery tanks in its right side. The detonating round got rid of the hover tank of its kaiju problem but also did a great deal of damage to the blower that kept it aloft. The hover tank's right side dropped to drag across the sand as its engine strained to compensate the loss of part of its hover system.

The sight of it floundering about, damaged, was all the incentive the kaiju near its position needed to take it down. They poured onto the tank, their claws raking its hull and leaving long, jagged grooves in it. Three of the kaiju worked together grasping the barrel of the tank's main gun and ripped it from the vehicle. The tank's engine must have given out from the strain because with a final shrieking whine, its blower stopped working and the tank plowed nose first into the sand to sit there unmoving, the swarm of kaiju attacking it ravaged its hull, tearing their way inside to get at its crew. Small arms fire rang out as the men inside the tank tried to fight back. It was a useless effort given the number of the kaiju but Campbell knew he would have done the same. No soldier ever just sat still and waited for death to take him if he could fight.

The kaiju pulled the remaining two members of the hover tank crew out of it and gutted them, while yanking their arms and legs from their bodies in a frenzy of spraying blood and gore. Campbell looked away as some of the kaiju began to feed upon their prey.

The Greenery tanks were firing full out now. The barrels of their main guns flashed in rapid succession firing as quickly as their auto-loader systems could deliver fresh rounds to them. Their barrage hammered the hover tanks bearing down on them. The shells were Old World ones like the tanks themselves. They were deadly yes but not powerful enough for a single shell to outright destroy a Tech-designed hover tank short of a very lucky hit. The Greenery tanks had the advantage for the moment though as the hover tanks were still being swarmed by the surviving kaiju. The hover tanks had thinned the number of the kaiju immensely, but there were dozens of the monsters that continued to come at them from all sides now that the creatures had closed with them.

As the Greenery's combat cars began to sweep forward, Campbell heard Major Leiber's voice over the comm.

"All mech units, engage those combat cars!" she ordered. "But hold back and do so from a distance."

The order was what Campbell had been waiting on. He had been dying to get into the action and here was his chance at last. He activated *Ragnarok Valkyrie*'s wrist-mounted rail-canons as the giant mech raised its arms to target the combat cars. With a sound akin to an unending crack of thunder, they opened up on the combat cars, hosing them with a stream of fire that instantly reduced two of them to exploding masses of shrapnel-like debris.

Hulking Diablo's eye-shaped panels on its head glowed red as they charged up before beams of energy pulsed downward from them to slice through a combat car's armor as if it were little more than wet paper. The combat car melted away into slag beneath the fury and power of the eye-beams.

Entropic Rush opened its giant hands as the flechette launchers in their center cycled open. The supersonic burst of the rounds leaving them created a small sonic boom as they streaked towards their targets. One of the two combat cars in the path of *Entropic Rush*'s line of fire tried to swerve clear of the incoming projectiles but all it really managed to do was present a wider target for the mech's fire. Both combat cars were cut to pieces in a fraction of a second, their crews slashed up into blood-smeared bits of meat with them.

Sand Stomper wasn't going to be outdone though. It was Major Leiber's personal mech and Campbell knew the lady had a rep to live up to. The giant Mech stomped its foot, sending a carefully aimed ground quake into the line of Greenery forces outside the city. The Greenery combat cars were hover vehicles like their own tanks so the quake had no effect on them but that hadn't been Major Leiber's intent. The quake slammed into a cluster of three Greenery tanks. The one in the quake's center flew into the air like a toy tossed aside by an angry child. It landed with its belly facing upwards for a brief second before it blew from the force of the impact. The other two tanks were jostled about and flung onto their sides as the quake rolled beneath them. Campbell could already see their crews scrambling out of them and running towards gates of the city behind them. The massive gates had been long been closed but there was nowhere else for them to run to.

****

War Leader Hoyt watched the men he shared the top of the city's wall with readying shoulder-mounted Swarm launchers at his command. The battle was going poorly and it would likely only be a matter of time until whoever was leading the Tech forces decided to let the mechs they had held in reserve truly enter the battle. Already, the mechs were making short work of the combat cars under his command. As yet, not a single combat car had even been able to get off a shot with their mech-killer missiles that found its target. Most of the cars had died before even getting the chance to launch one of the missiles at all. War

Leader Hoyt knew the city had no real defense against the mechs. Once the hulking machines came stomping towards Canton, the battle was as good as done. Surrender wasn't an option though. He reached out with his mind over the psi-link he shared with those under his command and thought, "All tank units, engage those mechs while they're dealing with the combat cars!"

The line of tanks assembled outside the city's walls hurried to follow his command. Their barrels rose upwards, targeting the mechs. A cacophony of thunder raged as the tanks began firing sporadically at their new targets. The explosions of detonating shells flashed against the armor of the mechs. The shells the old world tanks fired, however, lacked the power to do much damage to the hulking metal giants but War Leader Hoyt hoped they would get lucky. As their barrage continued to hammer into the mechs, one of them staggered backwards. It was the largest of the mechs. Its color matched that of the sand it stood on. War Leader Hoyt trained his vision enhancers on it. He could see that one of the tanks had indeed scored a lucky shot directly into the interlocking joint of the mech's right knee.

"Concentrate all fire on the largest mech," he amended his previous order. The Techs didn't fight fair so there was no reason he should either. The mechs were insanely costly things for the Techs to build. Intel suggested it took the techs six months or more to construct a single one of the hulking metal monsters. If he could bring one down, even just one, maybe the loss of Canton would be worth it. At the very least, he would have made the Techs pay for taking his city.

The tanks shifted their fire concentrating it all onto the single mech that had stumbled. The sand-colored giant fell back, disappearing beneath the flashing explosions of the tanks' combined fire. Some of the gunners in the tank must have seen the same thing he had because they were aiming for the mech's weakened knee. Another shell struck it at just the right angle and the mech's damaged knee gave out. The sand-colored mech half-dropped, half-fell onto the damaged knee, jerking its arms up to use as shields against the rain of shells that continued to hammer it. Those arms, while still mostly intact, were beginning to show signs of real damage now from the concentrated barrage pounding into them.

All four of the mechs were still out of range of the Swarm launchers the men on the wall around War Leader Hoyt held ready and the remaining few combat cars weren't having any better luck. They had managed to launch some of their side-mounted mech-killer missiles but none of them had made it through the mechs' defensive flak.

As War Leader Hoyt watched, a mech with the name *Entropic Rush* painted on its armored hull came bounding over to the sand-colored one's side. It targeted the line of tanks with a burst of flechette rounds that swept over their ranks. One tank after another blew in a cascading series of explosions. The surviving tanks broke formation, pulling out of the firing line, backing up towards the city. Two of them swerved about to make for the city gates while the only other remaining tank shot forward in a suicidal charge towards the mech that had slain its comrades. Its main gun boomed as it closed in on the mech named *Entropic Rush*. The charging tank's first shot covered the mech's right shoulder in flames. Its second slammed into the mech's chest with no visible effect. Seemingly more annoyed than truly threatened, *Entropic Rush* brought both its hands around to target the tank. The flechette launchers embedded in its palms reduced the charging tank to an unmoving mass of twisted and ravaged metal. The explosion that followed as the tank's onboard ammo went up blew what little remained of the tank into bits and pieces that went spinning away from the center of the blast.

Another of the mechs sprang forward, its eyes blazing. Beams of pure energy sliced downward from them at the two tanks making a run for the city gates. They cut the first tank apart along the middle of its armored body before it too blew up in an explosion that sent slagged chunks of metal bouncing across the sand. The second tank tried to dodge as the mech's eyes turned towards it. The creature that was its engine shrieked as it strained to pour on more speed but that cry was cut short as the mech's eye beams washed over the tank's main body, melting it and cooking those inside its armored body.

****

Major Leiber was screaming orders over the comm. as Campbell hurled *Ragnarok Valkyrie* into action. The ground seemed to shake from her footfalls as she stomped towards the city of Canton behind *Hulking Diablo*. The giant red mech had pulled the matching battle axes it carried on its hips from their magnetic locks and hefted them in its hands. *Ragnarok Valkyrie* was the faster of the two mechs but Campbell was more than happy to let Peter take the lead in *Hulking Diablo*. *Hulking Diablo* was the larger of the two of them and was more heavily armored. Peter and *Hulking Diablo* currently held the record for the highest number of kaiju kills for a single mech unit. If Peter wanted to go crashing into the city's wall and take the brunt of whatever defense forces was waiting for them there, Campbell was willing to let him do it.

Geddy, piloting *Entropic Rush*, had finished the last of the city's tanks and had taken up a defensive position next to where Major Leiber's mech, *Sand Stomper,* crouched. From the looks of *Sand Stomper*'s arms and right leg, the mech wasn't going anywhere. *Sand Stomper*'s right leg was nearly separated from the rest of its body at its knee. Sparks flew from the exposed wiring and servos there. *Sand Stomper*'s arms had taken a good beating too. They were spotted with ruptured patches of armor where the tanks' shells had worn through them and Campbell could see some minor fires dancing inside a few of those ruptured areas. Thick, black tendrils of smoke rose from *Sand Stomper* drifting upwards from where it crouched, their blackness matching that of Major Leiber's fury as her voice came over *Ragnarok Valkyrie*'s comm. again, so loudly that it caused him to flinch.

"Kill those bastards!" she spat. "I want that city burnt to the ground and everyone in it dead!"

At that moment, *Hulking Diablo* plowed into the wall that surrounded the city of Canton. An entire section of it crumpled under the fury of the giant mech, caving inward. *Hulking Diablo*'s axes swung in mighty arcs that hacked away at the rest of the city's north facing wall. The city's defenders there died by the dozens with each blow. Some falling to their deaths alongside the chunks of the wall that broke off and thudded onto the sand below; others smeared in gory stains beneath the blows of the mech's giant axes.

The awe and horror of the city's defenders on the wall changed to anger and determination as several two-man crews brought the Swarm launchers they had readied around to target *Hulking Diablo.* There was a series of popping noises as three of them fired in rapid succession.

"Look out!" Campbell shouted over the comm. at Peter.

Hulking Diablo's upper body shifted, partially turning, to try to dodge the beehive-shaped rounds streaking at it. The tactic prevented one of them from hitting it as it sailed passed the mech and onward into the empty air above the sand outside the city. The other two, however, made contact, bursting against the mech's armor to unleashed hordes of genetically engineered, metal-eating insects on it. One of the shells had burst on *Hulking Diablo*'s chest. Campbell could hear Peter cursing over the comm as a car-sized section of the red mech's armor seemed to evaporate as the insects went to work on it. The other shell covered one of *Hulking Diablo*'s axes with a mass of the insects. The axe was eaten away to where its shaft protruded from the mech's clutching fist and then spread onto the metal of *Hulking Diablo*'s fingers and hand.

Campbell jerked up *Ragnarok Valkyrie*'s wrist-mounted rail-cannons, hosing what was left of the top of the city's north-facing wall with streams of fire that massacred the remaining men and women defending the city, turning them in pulped masses of shredded human meat. And just like that, the battle was over as quickly as it had begun.

Whoever had been in command of the city of Canton's forces appeared to have held nothing in reserve. Campbell heard Peter still cursing inside *Hulking Diablo* as the red mech plunged onward into the city, kicking at random buildings and stomping the civilians who were trying to flee that were unlucky enough to find themselves in the mech's path.

****

Joster's heart leaped with joy when he spotted the abandoned Tech jeep on the horizon. It took all his self-control not to go just running towards it. The rational part of his brain told him that it might not really be abandoned at all. It could be a trap of some sort. He slowed his pace and ducked behind one of the large rocks that littered this part of the Waste. The Waste was what both his own people and the Techs called all of the world that was outside of their towns and cities. The Waste got its name from the lack of vegetation and clean water within it as much as it did for the fact that it was nothing but sand as far as the eye could see in any direction. Whatever had caused the fall of the Old World had left almost of all of the world this way he thought as snuck a peek around the edge of the rock he hid behind at the Tech jeep. Joster was no historian. He couldn't remember from his classes in school if the Waste had been born of the war that shattered the Old World or some great cataclysm that had caused the war in the first place. He supposed all that was the past anyway and didn't really matter much now regardless.

The jeep looked intact though its wheels were partially buried in the sand, as if the Waste had crept up onto the vehicle and was trying to pull it downward into the earth. There was no sign of any Techs about. Nonetheless, he waited, staring at the jeep for a solid ten minutes before he left the cover of the rock and started towards it again.

Approaching the jeep carefully, he eyed its ignition. No keys dangled there. Whoever had left the jeep behind had apparently taken those with them. The Tech jeep looked very similar to the Old World jeeps that the Greenery refit into its own service. Joster knew some about the Old World jeeps. The keys that were needed to start them worked in a sense like the button in a Greenery jeep. When one stabbed the ignition button in a Greenery jeep, a charge of electrical current was sent into the lifeform that acted as its power source telling the creature to activate its power generation. Joster wasn't entirely sure, but he suspected that the keys of a Tech jeep when turned caused a spark that activated the combustion of its completely mechanized engine. Tech jeeps ran on gasoline. Joster frowned as he remembered that fact. It meant this jeep was likely useless to him. Any gas left in its engine was surely evaporated or inert by now. Besides, he didn't have the keys needed to try to crank it and get it going anyway. He had heard of a process called hot-wiring that could be used to start such a vehicle when its keys were lost but he had no intention of attempting anything of the sort. For all he knew, had he pulled off the panel in front of the driver's seat and started playing around with the wires there, the whole jeep might blow up.

Still, stumbling onto the jeep was a blessing. He dug around through the bags in its rear and found a Tech grenade there. He shoved the grenade into his pocket after giving it a close examination to make sure he understood how it worked. Joster had certainly seen such grenades used against Greenery forces often enough. Further digging through the bags produced a bag of trail-mix. He tore into it at once, eating handfuls of it at a time as he continued his search of the jeep. It did wonders to stop the growling of his stomach and helped him shake some of the depression that had been weighing on him since he had started his lone trek through the Waste. He also found a battery-powered flashlight, a flare, and a half-full canteen of water. The water was rancid and had to be poured out but he kept the canteen. If he did somehow find more water out here, he would have a place to store it easily and safely.

The sun was nearly gone from the sky and the cold winds of the Waste night were beginning to howl over the sand. He sat in the jeep's driver seat, resting and piddling with the Tech flashlight. He turned it on once to make sure its batteries had power. They did. Once he saw that, he turned it back off, wanting to save whatever was left in them for a time when he really needed it. It looked like it was going to be a clear night as the sun finally disappeared altogether and the moon rose. The moon was full and bright, providing him with more than enough light to keep moving if he chose to. Joster was exhausted and the thought of staying in the jeep for the night caused him to linger at it. Sleeping in one of its seats would be much more comfortable than stretching out on the sand; safer too.

With a start, he realized he hadn't checked the jeep's glove box. Leaning over, he reached out to flip it open. His breath caught as he saw the gleam of metal inside it. An Old World revolver rested inside the glove box. Joster pulled it out and checked its chamber. The gun was fully loaded. Snapping its cylinder like chamber back in place, Joster didn't pocket the weapon. He kept it out and ready as he forced himself to get up out of the driver's seat. His legs were shaky for a moment, not wanting to support his weight. He steadied himself and took a second to get his bearings before setting out southward again. So far, he had been lucky not to run into any more Tech units on their way towards the Greenery's capital. He hadn't run into any of the predators that stalked the Waste either. There were *things* that lurked out here that were just as monstrous as the kaiju the Greenery bred as its weapons. Joster didn't know if the Tech pistol would be enough to protect him if he did encounter any of the predators of the Waste but he knew he was much better off having it than not.

He finished the final handful of trail-mix and tossed the empty plastic bag onto the wind. It blew away, fluttering, into the semi-darkness of the night. Joster washed it down with a slug of water from his supply he had carried with him from the scene of the battle. He didn't have much water left. The heat of the day had forced him to consume most of the pitiful amount he carried already.

Like every member of the Greenery's population, Joster was psi-sensitive to a degree. It was never something he had been exceptionally talented at, but he tried to reach out with his mind anyway. If there was a Greenery unit nearby, he hoped he would be able to at least feel if not link up with their shared psi-link. All he felt was emptiness though. Accepting his fate of being alone out here, he trudged onward over the sand, promising himself he would keep moving until he found help, made it home, or his legs gave out under him.

****

The trip to Councilor Sheehan's factory was a short one. Colonel Jaeger's hover car half-turned in the air as it slowed for its decent onto the exterior landing pad. Like all the other factories in Steel Heart, Councilor Sheehan's was a sprawling mass of black buildings, smoke stacks, reactor towers, and well-positioned lightning rods used to collect what additional energy they could from the storms that often raged above the city. None of the structures were as tall as the buildings of the Old World were shown to be in the history books that remained. Steel Heart had learned very quickly that the sky belonged to the Greenery. Despite their advances in helicopter tech and the development of winged power armor for the Steel Heart infantry troopers that guarded the city proper, nothing matched the agility, speed, and ferocity of the winged kaiju that the Greenery could unleash upon when such beasts were available. Thankfully, that wasn't very often, as intel suggested the flying monsters were more difficult to produce than even the giant true kaiju that were the Greenery's primary weapons of mass destruction. Even so, the Council of Engineers had opted to build downward, into the ground, instead of upwards into the sky. Less than half of the city was above ground and the bulk of the sections that were served either purposes that could be obtained in no other way or were military in nature.

The pilot landed the hover car and nodded into its rear, letting Colonel Jaeger and Major Steiner know that he was ready for them to disembark. Major Steiner led the way as the two of them got out of the car and headed across the landing platform to where four members of Councilor Sheehan's honor guard waited for them. Each of the guards wore full suits of power armor. Metal wings were retracted into the protruding bulge of the suits between the men's shoulders. The glowing yellow lenses that covered their eyes lit the growing darkness of the early evening. In their hands, they carried wicked-looking, shortened rifles out of the bottom of which curved banana-shaped magazines filled with rounds powerful enough to pierce the armor of an Old World tank. Strapped to their right hips were swords that dangled there in their sheaths. The swords were no ordinary blades but energy charged ones designed to slash through the thickened scales of kaiju flesh.

One of the guards who wore the rank of captain on his right arm of his suit stepped forward to meet them. Giving him an honorary half-bow, the guard said, "Welcome, Colonel Jaeger. Councilor Sheehan has been expecting your arrival."

Colonel Jaeger thought he detected the slightest trace of annoyance in the guard's voice as he spoke. No matter how advanced the suit he wore was, the man beneath it was still a human with all the baggage that came with being one. Likely, the captain and his squad had been waiting on them some time, as he hadn't exactly left his office in a mad rush to get here.

Doing his best to keep his own annoyance at being summoned to the factory like a commoner from showing, Colonel Jaeger answered, "A pleasure to visit as always, Captain. If you'd kindly lead the way, I am sure we have kept the councilor waiting long enough already."

The captain nodded and motioned for the other guards to remain where they were as he led Colonel Jaeger and Major Steiner into the factory. The massive exterior doors at the end of the landing platform slide open to admit them. The light of the corridor behind them made Colonel Jaeger blink as he entered it. The artificial lights glowed bright spilling out into the gloom surrounding the factory until the massive doors closed once more behind them.

"If you'll follow me, sir," the captain said, his armored feet clanging upon the metal of the corridor's floor as he walked. The three of them came to a lift. The captain stepped aside to allow Colonel Jaeger and Major Steiner to enter it. "This will take you directly to the outer portion of the councilor's office, sir."

"Thank you, Captain," Colonel Jaeger said in parting as the doors of the lift closed and it sprang into motion. There was sudden lurch, followed by a feeling of rapid decent, and then an equally sudden lurch as the lift came to a halt.

Colonel Jaeger and Major Steiner stepped out of the lift in the lobby of the councilor's office. Along its walls were pieces of Old World art that Colonel Jaeger could only speculate at in terms of their value. Each of them had a priceless vibe to it. Much of the art depicted a well-muscled but beautiful woman dressed in the clothes of an Old World factory worker. Often the words, "She can do it!" were printed upon the painting in bold script. Major Steiner paused to admire one of the pieces of art with a wry grin.

"I wonder what he sees in this stuff," the major commented, staring up at a print of a woman with long dark hair wielding a sword as she crouched in a combat stance, ready for to slice whatever opponent she may face in half.

"Come on," Colonel Jaeger ordered. "We didn't come here to appraise the councilor's taste in women."

Major Steiner gave a half-snort, half-giggle, turning away from the print that had so caught his attention, and followed him to the doors of the councilor's office at the end of the hall. As they approached, the entrance to the office dilated open to admit them.

Councilor Sheehan sat behind his desk, reading what appeared to be called a "comic book" in the Old World. Colonel Jaeger had no doubt that it was real and likely cost as much as the hover car he had flown to the factory in.

Noticing the two of them, Councilor Sheehan lifted what appeared to a protective plastic sleeve from the top of his desk and carefully eased the book he had been reading into it before properly addressing them.

"Colonel Jaeger!" he exclaimed jubilantly. "I am so glad you decided to accept my request to drop by for a visit."

"Cut the chit-chat, Councilor," Colonel Jaeger said firmly in what he hoped wasn't too gruff of a tone. "Get to whatever you needed me here for. The battle for the Greenery's city of Canton is likely concluding as we speak and I am needed elsewhere."

"I see." Councilor Sheehan frowned deeply. "I am sorry to have called you away from such important matters, Colonel, but once you have seen what I have to show you, I think you'll understand why I sent for you, and you alone, so urgently."

"But I am not alone," Colonel Jaeger pointed out, gesturing at Major Steiner.

Councilor Sheehan chuckled. "The major here is of no concern. I believe him to be one of the most loyal soldiers in Steel Heart's army, Colonel Jaeger. If someone such as myself can't trust men like him, then perhaps all that is of true value is lost already."

"And what is it that you have the need to show me so urgently?" Colonel Jaeger growled, trying to keep Councilor Sheehan focused.

Councilor Sheehan raised his pointer finger with a wide smile, adding an overly dramatic element to the gesture for Colonel Jaeger's taste before he stabbed a button on his desk and the wall behind it began to slide apart to reveal a large window. The view through the window looked down on a mech building pit. Almost all of Steel Heart's mechs were constructed underground in chambers like the one Colonel Jaeger found himself staring into. The thing was that each factory was only allowed two mech pits. He knew this one wasn't one of the two that Councilor Sheehan's factory had registered with the Council of Engineers and the military offices.

"I call her Samurai One." Councilor Sheehan grinned at him. "She's the first of her kind. She's a class-seven Mech," he added proudly.

"Class seven?" Colonel Jaeger repeated the words as he approached the window behind the desk to get a better look at the portion of the mech that was visible through it. Samurai One looked like any other mech that Colonel Jaeger had seen in his career. She did have a very distinctive flare to her though. The bulk of what he could see of her body was blue tapered with black and silver streaks. Her head was rounded and sunk into her heavy shoulders, the armored blades of which extended like the armor worn by the warriors that were her namesake.

Major Steiner appeared as surprised by this development as he was as Colonel Jaeger stole a glance at the younger officer.

"Do you have any idea how illegal this is?" Colonel Jaeger stammered in disbelief. Councilor Sheehan was either a madman to show him this mech or trusted him implicitly. To expend Steel Heart's limited resources on a project of this scope without consent from the Council of Engineers and the military was a crime punishable by death. If Colonel Jaeger reported this mech's existence, it would be the end of Councilor Sheehan's career and his life. His factory would be seized by the military and held until a new administrator was assigned to it while Councilor Sheehan himself would be arrested and brought before the council for judgement that could surely only end with his death … and likely a painful one at that.

Councilor Sheehan laughed. "I know full well the risks I have taken to build Samurai One colonel. Building her has taken everything I have. In my opinion, she is worth it all though and more. I know you desperately want to end the war with the Greenery. The other members of the Council of Engineer are aware of just how deeply that desire burns within you too. No soldier can win a war though without the proper weapons at his or her disposal, however."

"You're insane," Major Steiner muttered just loudly enough for the two of them to hear. The young major's face had gone pale and his right hand rested dangerously close to the butt of the pistol holstered on his hip.

"Major," Colonel Jaeger called for the young man's attention. Major Steiner looked in his direction and their eyes met as Colonel Jaeger gave a sharp shake of his head, warning the young man not to do anything rash.

"Have a seat, Major Steiner," Councilor Sheehan ordered, gesturing at one of the chairs in front of his desk. "The colonel and I have much to discuss. We'll likely be at it for a good while."

Colonel Jaeger nodded his consent at Major Steiner, telling him to do as the councilor instructed at least for the time being. Major Steiner must have realized that his fingers had slipped onto the butt of his pistol and he was now clutching the weapon. He jerked his hand free of it as if blazing stove eye.

"Sorry, sir," Major Steiner sulked, his shoulders slumping as he took the seat the councilor had directed him to.

Colonel Jaeger returned his full attention to Councilor Sheehan. "You say she's a class seven? What exactly does that mean, Councilor?"

"Each generation of mech that climbs out of our building pits exceeds their predecessors in some fashion. They're faster, more responsive, more agile, more heavily armored, or are perhaps sporting some new type of weapon that we engineers hope will turn the tide of the war with the Greenery. Class-five mechs were the toughest mechs ever built. They were strong enough to go hand to hand with the Greenery's great kaiju and yank the monsters' spines from their living bodies. Class-six mechs were the best all-around ever produced. Their abilities in terms of speed, response times, etc. were the closest to natural human movements that our technology would allow us to create at the time. And the class-six mechs have served Steel Heart well, very well in fact."

"I didn't ask for a history lesson, Councilor," Colonel Jaeger pressed Councilor Sheehan for a more direct and to the point answer as what the capabilities of the class seven in the pit behind and below the office were.

"I suppose you didn't at that, Colonel." Councilor Sheehan sighed. "I sometimes forget that unlike many of the high-ranking officers in our military today, you were a mech pilot for a time. How you could ever give up such a thing …"

"It's a mystery to me too sometimes, Councilor. If I said I didn't miss it, I would be lying," Colonel Jaeger admitted. "But Steel Heart needed a leader who would end the war with the Greenery once and for all. You and your peers seem to believe I am that leader since you granted me my current position."

"Indeed," Councilor Sheehan wholeheartedly agreed. "We wanted someone who wouldn't be bogged down by long-standing military doctrine. Someone who would think outside of the box and do whatever it took to bring the conflict to an end in our time. Your ability to do those things combined with the risks you've already pressed the Council of Engineers into taking after your appointment are exactly why I felt I could show you Samurai One."

"And you truly believe I won't simply leave this office and turn you in for what you've done here?" Colonel Jaeger asked his disbelief still clear in his voice.

"You won't, Colonel." Councilor Sheehan smiled. "And I will tell you why. The mech you see before you, she's not only faster, more agile, and more human like in her movements than any ever constructed before, but she can fly too."

Colonel Jaeger's eyes bugged in complete shock as he jerked his head around to look at Samurai One in her building pit again.

Major Steiner leaped up from his chair, the palms of his hands slapping down onto the top of the councilor's desk as he exclaimed, "That's impossible!"

"Oh, but is it now?" Councilor Sheehan smirked. "Once, yes, certainly that was true, but no longer. I assure you, gentlemen, that Samurai One is fully flight-capable."

"How?" Colonel Jaeger rasped, barely getting the words out.

"The how isn't as important as that she does," Councilor Sheehan told them. "I'll be happy to provide you a full copy of her specifications, Colonel. You'll want to find her a pilot capable of handling her and get her into the field as quickly as possible. I know that, like myself, you believe the rumors that the Greenery has found a means of mass producing the great kaiju on a scale we've never seen before. If they have discovered such a process, it likely means the end for all of Steel Heart unless we act now to stop them before this new process bears fruit and we are overrun. I have no desire to see our beliefs and way of life wiped from the face of this planet by those genetically mutated madmen. That is why I risked everything to build her, Colonel, and why I am now coming clean to you so that you can put her to the use that she was built for."

"Who else knows about Samurai One?" Colonel Jaeger asked after a brief moment of thought.

"Aside from the three of us, only the most loyal and trusted of my employees here at the factory. I handpicked every person who had a hand in her construction, Colonel, and can assure you that no one will know of her existence until you are ready to put her to use. My word on that." Councilor Sheehan smiled.

"Clearly, they can be trusted or all of Steel Heart would know about a project like this one by now." Major Steiner nodded, suddenly backing up the councilor despite his earlier rage at the man's deception. "A flying mech, sir," he said turning to Colonel Jaeger, "and one better designed than our best class-six models … She could change everything if she's truly as combat effective as Councilor Sheehan appears to be implying that she is."

"Agreed," Colonel Jaeger said, more to keep the young major calm than anything else.

"So, Colonel Jaeger, I must ask," Councilor Sheehan eyed him, "am I to be placed under arrest or have we reached an understanding, an alliance if you will?"

"You're not under arrest, Councilor Sheehan … at least not yet," Colonel Jaeger answered reluctantly. "I'll be wanting that copy of her specs you offered. You have given me a look to think about."

Councilor Sheehan was grinning smugly again. "Here," he said, walking over to press a flashdrive into Colonel Jaeger's hand. "Contact me when you have a pilot for her. No one will know she even exists until you are ready for them to. Again, you have my word on that."

Holding tightly to the flashdrive, Colonel Jaeger nodded and started for the office door. "Major, it's time we were gone from here. The battle for the city of Canton is surely over by now and there's much we need to check in on and do."

The two of them left the councilor alone in his office, staring after them with his hands clasped behind him as they went. Colonel Jaeger wasn't quite sure if he had been delivered the answer to his prayers or plunged into a nightmare from which there would be no coming back.

****

Grand Doula Minerva walked along the winding curves of the ledge above the hatchery. Four escorts walked with her. The Grand Doula seldom went anywhere outside of her chambers alone. Three of them were either more or less than human depending on how one viewed such things. One of them was a female with cat-like eyes that almost seemed to glow a feral shade of red in the dim light of the hatchery. A tail protruded from her back just above her buttocks. Her movements bore an inhuman grace as she sauntered along after the Grand Doula. Another had the snout and scaled skin of a crocodile. Her thick muscles bulged beneath the fabric of the thin tunic she wore. Her razor-like teeth clicked together ever so softly as she walked, ready to tear into any prey that chose to present itself. The final of the Grand Doula's more bizarre guardians was covered in brown fur from head to toe. She wore no clothes and her soft feet made no sound as they moved across the floor. Between her arms and the upper torso of her body were leathery wings, folded up neatly within that space. Her ears were pointed and stretched upwards from her head, more than twice the size of a normal human's. Eyes locked into a permanent squint above the stub of a nose that rested in the center of her face, she sniffed at the air of the hatchery, ever on guard against any threat that might dare to enter the sacred chamber.

The Grand Doula's fourth escort appeared out of place amidst the others. He was a strikingly handsome man with long golden hair that lay draped over his wide shoulders. His eyes were a sharp contrast to the rest of him. He appeared young, perhaps in his early twenties, but his eyes held an eerily ancient depth to them that bespoke his true age. He wore a well-tailored, business suit, entirely white in its color from his jacket to the boots upon is feet. To glance at him amidst the horror he accompanied, he would certainly seem the least threatening to those who didn't know who and what he was. His name was Denkirch and was the Doula Mate, second-in-command of the Greenery. Though genetic alterations made him far stronger and faster than a normal human male, his real strength resided within his mind. All citizens of the Greenery possessed some margin of psychic power or sensitivity. Denkirch's went far beyond that norm, however. He was a telekinetic of the highest order. With the sheer strength of his mind and his will, Denkirch could rend metal and oh so much more.

Grand Doula Minerva, paused turning to lean over the ledge's railing and peer down into the depths of the Hatchery itself. There was a time, not very long ago at all, when the Hatchery below would be home to little more than half a dozen man-sized eggs. Now its entire floor was covered with them. The eggs pulsed with bio-energy that crackled up their sides and over them, blue lightning dancing like flames. She drank in the sight of her kaiju children on the verge of being born. Soon, they would rip their way free of their shells and their inborn growth acceleration would kick in. Within a day, perhaps two, they would reach their full towering heights. Kaiju of their type would grow to stand between two hundred and three hundred feet tall. They were the Greenery's great weapons in the war against the Techs.

There were close to four dozen eggs covering the Hatchery floor. They were more than enough once born to bring about the end to the Greenery's enemies once and for all. The Grand Doula's seers assured her that the Techs had no more than ten of their kaiju slayer mechs operational and were nowhere close to finishing the construction of more of the hulking metal monsters. Those mechs would be outnumbered more than three to one when the time for the final battle of the long-running war came to be waged.

She gave a start as she noticed that Doula Mate Denkirch had joined her in leaning on the railing. Her senses both psychically and physically were so advanced beyond those a mere human's that she was not used to someone slipping up on her unnoticed.

"I am sorry, Grand Doula," her mate apologized. "It was not my intent to frighten you."

Giving a sharp hiss, Grand Doula Minerva whirled on Denkirch. "You dare think that you can frighten one such as I?"

Denkirch backed away from her, his hands spread, open palmed in a gesture of submission and surrender. "I didn't mean to offend, Grand Doula. I pray you will forgive your mate for his poor choice of words."

Doula Mate Denkirch was powerful enough to challenge her and she knew it. For all his power though, she remained supreme. A fight between the two of them would shake the very foundations of the Greenery. With victory over the Techs so close at hand, she was willing to forgive a number of such transgressions, but Denkirch was beginning to push her to her limits. Her mate was as arrogant and ambitious as he was handsome and strong.

Suddenly, her anger was masked behind a smile that showed her fang-like teeth. "You forget your place again, my love, and not even your skills at pleasuring me will save you from what you deserve," she purred, reaching out to run her fingers over the side of his right cheek. They pressed tighter against his flesh as they swept down the curve of his cheek, drawing blood at the last instant before they parted from it.

Pulling away from her and taking a step backwards from her position at the ledge's railing, Doula Mate Denkirch wiped at the blood now dripping from where her claws had marked him. He stared at her in shock. Grand Doula Minerva could feel the anger seething within him but he said nothing more. Denkirch merely nodded and backed even farther away.

"There may come a time that you truly decide to challenge me, Denkirch, but it will not be today," she said firmly. "There is too much at stake for us all for such petty bickering over power to put it all at risk. The future of the Greenery must take precedence. Even now as we speak, the Techs push farther and farther into our domain. The two of us must remain united until they have been driven from our land and crushed beneath the scaled feet of our children."

"Yes, Grand Doula," Denkirch answered though she would be a fool to believe that his agreement was heartfelt.

A trio of women dressed in bright red robes approached their party from the other side of the ledge above the Hatchery. They were the leaders of the kaiju mothers. Their job was to oversee the kaiju during the hatching process and assure that the kaiju grew both as intended and as quickly as possible.

The tallest of the ladies in the red bowed deeply to her as the Grand Doula moved to meet them.

"My lady," the kaiju mother said. "What brings you by? We have heard the stories of the Techs' push into our lands. Is the Hatchery truly at risk?"

The Grand Doula's lips parted in the beginnings of a snarl but that snarl abruptly melted in a wide smile. Her voice was calm and controlled as she spoke. "You and your mothers have no reason to fear, Mother Gretch. No Tech shall ever set foot within these sacred walls."

"That is good to hear." Mother Gretch smiled back at her. "By this time tomorrow, our new batch of children shall be born and growing towards adulthood. They are many, however, and their needs are great, so I am afraid I cannot linger to show more of just how blessed we are to have them."

"I understand, Mother." The Grand Doula nodded formally. "Use your time as you must. I have no doubt that these will our strongest warriors yet."

Mother Gretch bowed again in response to the formal compliment and then turned about, the other two kaiju mothers following her as they disappeared in the direction they had emerged from.

"Tomorrow," Grand Doula Minerva cackled wildly. "Tomorrow, the tide of this war will turn and the Techs will not only be driven back but in the days thereafter, the streets of Steel Heart will run with blood."

****

Joster could sense that he was no longer alone. Something was following him across the sands of the Waste. He was so tired it took all his will to keep moving. His sweat-slicked fingers held tight to the Tech revolver he had looted from the abandoned jeep he had stumbled upon. Joster held the weapon ready, as it was his only means of defense against whatever it was that followed him. His lungs ached as he sucked in another breath. Part of him wanted to lay down in the sand and surrender to what fate had in store for him no matter what it may be. He had been on the move for so long now that rest of any kind was all he wanted almost to point of accepting his final one if that was the only choice left open to him.

The Waste was home to many things, not all of them human. Yes, there were scattered tribes of nomads that roamed the sands, left over from the Old World and caught between the warring city-states of the Greenery and Steel Heart, but surely if it was a human pursuing him, he or she would have made their move by now. His haggard muscles tensed tighter as he thought of the wild kaiju who also called the Waste their home. He knew that none of the wild kaiju were true kaiju. They were of the smaller breeds, the ones bred to engage Tech infantry or perhaps merely to serve as cannon fodder.

Wild kaiju were truly frightening things. Gone was any semblance of control that those of the Greenery once had over them. The beasts were no longer bound by the psychic commands issued to them except but by the most powerful of telepathic senders. They were creatures of instinct who only cared about their next meal and remaining alive and free. Joster knew full well that he lacked the degree of psi-power to control such a beast or likely even convince it that he wasn't food to be shredded by its fangs and claws. The wild kaiju were completely unrestrained in their aggression and more fierce than even the best of the Greenery's warrior kaiju of their size.

Joster came to a stop where he was, his shoulders sagging from the lack of strength to hold them upright. He turned about, his tired eyes scanning the darkness of night for any sign of his pursuer. His guts went cold as he saw the pair of yellow, glowing eyes flash in the distance before they disappeared behind one of the large rocks that lay about in this section of the Waste. His worst fear confirmed, he thought of raising the barrel of the Tech revolver to his temple and ending it all right then and there. Doing so would at least spare him the effort and pain that would surely come when the kaiju grew bored of playing with him and moved in for the kill.

His best guess, based on how high the eyes appeared to glow above the sand in the brief moment he had glimpsed them, put the wild kaiju at standing roughly seven feet tall at its shoulders. The Tech revolver he knew contained six rounds but he had no clue as to what kind of stopping power the weapon had. He doubted it was enough to stop such a creature, even if fired all six of them into it. Attempting to make a run for it would be equally as useless more so given that he could barely keep himself on his feet as it was. The beast would easily overtake him if it had the desire to.

Joster kept as still he could, his gaze fixed on the rock that the wild kaiju had taken cover behind. There seemed to be nothing else to do but wait for the monster to make its move as he discovered he didn't have the courage to use the Tech weapon on himself. He raised the Tech revolver in the direction of where the creature was hiding. When it did show itself, he would be ready.

He didn't have to wait long. With a roar that seemed to shake the night, the wild Kaiju emerged from behind the boulder. It didn't come around one of the sides of the boulder, it came over it. The wild kaiju leaped onto the boulder's top and then to the ground in front of it, charging at Joster. He felt warm liquid running down over his legs as his balder released itself and he squeezed the revolver's trigger. The weapon's barrel flashed. The bullet smacked into the center of the kaiju's chest. Yellow blood spurted from where the bullet entered the creature's flesh. Shocked the shot had gotten penetration, Joster realized the revolver must be loaded with armor-piercing rounds. He squeezed the trigger several times again in rapid succession as the wild kaiju closed on him. His second and third shots dug into the wild kaiju's chest near where the first had struck the monster. The kaiju gave a pained screech and stumbled in its run. His fourth shot made contact with the softer flesh of the monster's throat. In an explosion of yellow fluid, it tore a gaping hole there. The kaiju's screech was cut short, becoming a sickening gurgling sound as it shook its head about, slinging blood over the sand in the process. The monster had stopped its advance. That was the important thing. Steadying his two-handed grip on the Tech revolver, Joster aimed his fifth shot carefully. He put a bullet directly between the monster's glowing eyes, and at last, it toppled over. Its body lay twitching on the sand, a pool of yellow forming around its thrashing form.

Standing there watching the kaiju die, Joster couldn't believe his luck. By all rights, he should be dead. Somehow, he had pulled himself out of the fire though and it was the kaiju that had been sent to Hell in his place. Tendrils of white smoke snaked upwards from the Tech revolver's barrel. He was tempted to walk over to the kaiju and use his last round to put it out of its misery and make sure the thing was dead. He didn't though. The monster was clearly dying. It was only a matter of time. Joster didn't dare turn his back on the creature so he stood there until it was completely still and he was sure that it had passed on. Only then did he lower his weapon and wipe the sweat from his brow. There was nothing he could about his urine-drenched pants except allow them to dry as he continued his journey southward.

"Nice shooting, son," a voice called out to him from the darkness.

Joster whirled about jerking up the revolver again the direction the voice had come from. Beneath the light of the moon and stars, he saw an older man standing nearby. The man wore an outfit of leathery armor that looked to be composed of kaiju hide. There was a double-barreled shotgun strapped to his back and a machete sheathed on his right hip. In his hands, he carried a spear with a wooden shaft and a piece of jagged steel that served as its head.

"Stay where you are," Joster warned the old man.

"Easy, boy," the old man warned him in return. "If I wanted you dead, you would be dead. I've been following you and that kaiju for the better part of an hour."

Joster's eyes bugged at the old man claim.

"I was already tracking him," the old man gestured at the kaiju's corpse, "and about to close in for the kill when he got your scent and took off after you. I suppose I should thank you for killing him for me. Saves me some effort." The old man smirked.

Joster still kept his revolver trained on the old man.

"Put that gun down and we'll get us some dinner going. I don't plan on keeping all of him for myself." The old man laid his spear on the sand, drawing a large knife that was sheathed to the side of one of his boots. As he rose up, Joster saw him glance at the Tech revolver.

"Don't make me ask you again, son," the old man said. "There's no reason more blood needs to be spilled this night."

Joster lowered the revolver and croaked, "Who are you?"

"You can call me Worm," the old man laughed. Seeing how uneasy Joster remained, he asked, "You're from the Greenery, aren't you? Defense force, right?"

Joster nodded.

"Yet you're carrying a Tech weapon," the old man commented. "I guess that means you're either a traitor or your unit got its butt kicked so bad you ended up out here in the middle of nowhere on your own. I'm guessing the second. That sound about right?"

"I was part of a convoy headed for the capital," Joster answered. "We were hauling a shipment of bio-gel. They hit us hard and fast. Most of us died. When those who did live through the attack pulled out, I was left behind."

"And now you're trying to get home," the old man said. Joster realized it wasn't a question but a knowing statement.

"Yeah, I am." Joster frowned.

"You look like Hell warmed over, son," the old man told him. "How long have you been out here walking?"

Joster just shrugged. He had lost all track of time.

The old man set to starting a fire out of scattered bits of long dead wood he dug up from the sand. It ignited easily as Joster watched him.

"This portion of the Waste used to be a sort of oasis for a while. There was a pool of water over there that bubbled up out of the sand. It was enough for some real vegetation to grow here for a time. This wood is from the small trees that were just beginning their life when your war swept through here. Don't really understand what happened but something, whether it was the earthshaking from all the mechs and kaiju or some unintended missile strike in just the right spot, but the water dried up."

Joster didn't have a clue what to say so he continued to watch the old man as he left the crackling fire and moved to the kaiju's corpse.

"You ever ate kaiju, boy?" The old man knelt next to the dead monster and sliced off a section of the creature's hide to get at the meat under it. He cut away a long strip and carried it back to the fire. "Not as bad as you'd think. Kind of tough but then so is life. At any rate, it'll keep you alive and that's what matters."

The old man took a seat, cross-legged by the fire, cooking the kaiju meat over it on a short metal rod he had taken out of the pack he had shrugged from his back and sat next to him along the double-barreled shotgun he had removed from his person as well.

Joster took a seat across the fire from him. He kept his pistol out and ready but made sure to hold it in as non-threatening a way as he could.

"You live out here?" Joster finally asked. The smell of the cooking meat had set his mouth to watering and his stomaching rumbling.

"Not everybody is either from the Greenery or a Tech, son," the old man snorted.

"Everyone that matters is," Joster said unable to stop the words from coming out. He was half-afraid the old man would try to kill him for saying them.

"Maybe." The old man flashed him a wry grin. "Your Greenery and the folks in Steel Heart certainly have the power and the numbers, but that don't necessarily mean as much as you think it does. I like to think that when the two of you of finally killed each other off, my kind will still be out here, living life and shaking our heads at just how crazy you both were."

"Crazy?" Joster asked, anger flaring up inside him.

"I'm living on wild kaiju meat, son, baking in the sun every day, while you live in a city where miracles happen yet all you and your people do is make war instead of enjoying what you have. Tell me, what is sane about that?"

"We don't have a choice," Joster challenged him. "The Techs would wipe us out if we didn't fight back."

"Aye," the old man nodded, "and you would do the same to them. Let me ask you this, boy, why? The Greenery and Steel Heart both are raping what's left of this world and for what? War? Wouldn't all that time and energy be better spent on making this world whole again?"

"That's what we're trying to do!" Joster exclaimed.

The old man shook his head. "No, son, it isn't. Not really. You folks in the Greenery think you're better than everyone else. Heck, a good portion of you ain't even human anymore. All that matters to you 'bettering' the human race because you think the rest of the world should be like you and if they aren't, well, then they aren't real humans anyway. I'd wager you Greenery folks don't have even a fraction of a clue what humanity really is or is all about. I can tell you it sure ain't making yourself into animals and plants like you folks do with your vaunted genetics."

The old man had crossed the line from being insulting to outright blasphemy. "So you're saying the Techs are right?"

"Hell no, son!" the old man shouted. "Their way of polluting everything in the name of progress and replacing what green is left in this world with iron and steel is just as bad. They've lost their souls to their machines and gadgets just as much as the Greenery has abandoned their souls to a vain quest for genetic perfection."

"Then which side are you on then?" Joster asked.

The old man looked him in the eye and said, "I'm on my own side, boy. I believe in freedom, God, and being true to one's self. Those are the things that really matter in life, not whether you can graft cat eyes into your head so you can see in the dark better or stick bits of circuitry into your skin so you can interface with some lifeless A.I. or giant robot body."

"I don't understand," Joster admitted.

"I suppose you wouldn't, boy." The old man sighed. "It's not a quest for perfection through genetics or machines either one that makes us who we are. We're born as we were meant to be. It's as plain and simple as that. We've all only got one life to live, and I would rather spend mine living it than taking the lives of others over something as pointless as either of your ideologies. If the powers that be of your Greenery and those in the fortress city of Steel Heart could understand that, well, this Waste would likely have long been healed and the world would be a better place to live in, now wouldn't it?"

The old man took a piece of the kaiju meat which had apparently finished cooking and handed to it. "Here. Eat it. You're going to need the strength."

Joster accepted the meat. Looking it over, it wasn't really something he wanted to put in his mouth but it smelled heavenly to his empty stomach. Joster took a small bite, grease from the meat washing over his tongue. Despite how it looked, it tasted as good as it smelled. He scarfed the rest of the meat down so quickly he swallowed chunks of it whole.

"Slow down." The old man frowned, handing him another piece. "Ain't gonna do you no good if you eat it so quick it just comes up again."

"Thank you," Joster managed to get out around a second mouthful of kaiju meat.

The old man produced a silver flask from the lining of the kaiju hide he wore, taking a long slug from it. When he was done, he offered it to Joster who accepted it eagerly.

Whatever was in the flask burned at Joster's throat like liquid fire. He made a pained face as he lowered the flask from his lips.

"Good, ain't it?" the old man reached to slap him on the shoulder. "Found it in the bowels of an almost ripped-in-half mech a few weeks ago."

"Now you get some rest, son," the old man urged him. "I'll keep watch. The sun will be up before we know it."

Joster didn't argue. Something deep down assured him that he could trust the old man. As crazy as he might seem, he didn't strike Joster as a man who killed without reason. Joster knew he had nothing of value except the Tech weapon and its last, single bullet. Surely that wasn't worth a human life.

Stretching out on the sand next to the fire, Joster closed his eyes. His exhaustion dragged him into sleep almost the moment they were closed.

****

As the sun began its ascent into the sky, the city of Canton, or rather what remained of it, was still burning. Major Leiber had stayed true to her word in having Taskforce Beta burn it to nothingness. Campbell sat on the hood of an ammo truck, watching the flames. A large group of Steel Heart infantry and support vehicles had caught up to the taskforce in the night. Much of the night had been spent reorganizing the taskforce's ranks to accommodate them, repairing damage done to the mechs and surviving hover tanks from the battle, and reloading the mechs and tanks alike.

Geddy, inside *Entropic Rush*, had stayed in his mech to watch over Taskforce Beta in case a unit of Greenery forces showed themselves seeking revenge for the loss of the city. Normally, more than one mech would have been on watch, but intel suggested that there were no kaiju in the area and a single mech was enough to go up against any rag-tag forces that might be dumb enough to try something after the defeat of Canton.

Repair personnel swarmed over *Sand Stomper* like human ants. Major Leiber oversaw their work, barking orders at them and flying into random rages when they attempted to adjust something on the mech that she didn't feel needed monkeyed with. Pilots often developed a very personal and deep connection to their mechs and Major Leiber, despite her rank, it seemed was no exception. From the look of things, the repair personnel were going to be able to get *Sand Stomper* close to fully operational. The damage to the mech's right leg had been extensive. There was no means of fixing up all the damage in the field but she was going to be mobile at least. Of course, given that *Sand Stomper*'s main weapon system was based in its legs, its combat effectiveness was going to be greatly reduced. Campbell couldn't help but wonder that if it had been any of the other mechs that were damaged in such a severe fashion if they would have been sent back to Steel Heart for proper repairs. *Sand Stomper* was Major Leiber's though, and as thus, it would be continuing on with the rest of Taskforce Beta for the Greenery's capital.

Peter leaned against the ammo truck next to where Campbell was sitting, puffing on a cigar. "Those Greenery freaks put up a better fight than I thought they would."

Campbell sighed. "Still didn't mean we had to kill them all."

"You sound like Geddy," Peter grunted. "We're soldiers, buddy. It's our job to kill folks."

Campbell knew better than to try to reason with someone with like Peter so he changed the subject. "If you think they put up a good fight here, imagine what taking their capital is going to like."

"It'll be epic," Peter laughed.

Sliding off the hood of the ammo truck, Campbell jumped to the ground next to Peter. "That's one way to put it, I guess."

Peter exhaled a cloud of smoke. "I know you don't like me, Campbell. Heck, I will admit I think you can be a bit of a pansy sometimes, but the long and short of it is that we're on the same side. We don't need to like each other. We just need to work together enough to get the job that needs doing done."

Campbell shot Peter a look at the pansy comment but opted to let it slide. Peter was right. All that mattered was ending the war and as soon as possible.

"Reckon we'll be rolling out as soon as the repairs to Leiber's mech are done," Peter said around the butt of the cigar stuck between his lips. "Best get back to our rides, eh?"

Campbell nodded and started walking towards *Ragnarok Valkyrie* as Peter tossed what was left of his cigar onto the sand, heading for *Hulking Diablo*.

Taskforce Beta was on the move again in less than an hour. A screen of forward-hover tanks skirted over the sand as the four mechs trudged along behind them. The infantry and support vehicles remained at the ruins of Canton. Major Leiber wanted them held back and out of direct contact with the enemy. They were assets that didn't need to be risked in order to achieve the goal that lay ahead of them.

"Hey, Campbell," Geddy called over the comm. "You picking up anything weird out there?"

Campbell checked *Ragnarok Valkyrie*'s sensors. "There's some sort of distortion field about ten miles out. Wait, no. It's nine miles out."

"That's what I mean, man. What that thing is, it's coming for us and fast," Geddy said.

"All mech units, full alert," Major Leiber interrupted them. "We've got incoming."

Campbell honed in a visual image of the distortion. "Frag!" he cursed.

"You see them too then?" Geddy asked.

"Of course I see them!" Campbell shouted.

"Good, because I thought I might be losing it," Geddy said in a way that made Campbell think the man was only half-joking. Geddy had always been an odd one. How he ever ended up a mech pilot was beyond Campbell's understanding. The man struck him as being much better suited to a career as an artist of some kind. Geddy was quick-witted, creative, and more than a little crazy sometimes.

The swarm of winged kaiju soared through the otherwise empty sky on a direct course for the Taskforce. The creatures of the swarm came in all shapes and sizes. Some of them looked like giant bats. Others reminded Campbell of the dragons out of the myths of the Old World. All of them though were clearly intent on tearing the quartet of mechs apart. Their screeches and inhuman cries could be heard even through the armor of his mech as Campbell brought up *Ragnarok Valkyrie*'s wrist cannons towards them. He was already firing as Major Leiber yelled, "All mech units, fire at will!"

A barrage of flechettes from *Entropic Rush* and cannon fire from *Ragnarok Valkyrie* hammered into the approaching swarm shredding kaiju flyers by the dozens. Most the kaiju that were hit burst apart in sprays of gore that fell like rain from the air over the sand. A few took indirect hits though that blew away parts of their bodies while leaving the rest of them intact. Those creatures fought madly to stay aloft. A good number of them ended up in spinning downwards to land on the sand where they picked themselves up with the limbs remaining to them and dragged their bodies onward towards the mechs. The Taskforce's forward screen of hover tanks opened fire on those creatures, their main guns making short work of them.

Despite Campbell and Geddy's efforts, however, there were just too many of the things to stop completely. The swarm came diving into towards the giant four mechs. *Hulking Diablo* cut one of the flyers in half with a swing of its right-handed axe while it blocked the attack of another with the axe in its left hand, knocking the flyer into a sideways spin that carried it away from the mech. Major Leiber in *Sand Stomper* deployed its shoulder mounted missile launchers. Six missiles streaked from each of them into the kaiju flyers. Not all the missiles detonated on impact. Some of them simply ripped through the flesh of the kaiju they struck and continued onward through the air, leaving those kaiju with their guts hanging out and their shrieks of violence changed to death cries of unimaginable pain. The missiles that did detonate blew the kaiju they made contact with into bits of pulped meat. Those missiles were *Sand Stomper*'s only real means of air defense, and with them gone, the battle became a lot more personal for Major Leiber. One of *Sand Stomper*'s massive hands snatched a kaiju from the air and crushed it to a yellow stain within the mech's clenched fist. By then, the kaiju were hitting back.

Campbell cursed as he tried to dodge an attack from one of the creatures, jerking the top half of *Ragnarok Valkyrie*'s body to the right. The kaiju's claws still managed to glance against the mech's armor as it passed by. Sparks flew as the claws parted the metal of the mech's shoulder in series of long grooves. The damage was mostly superficial. The claws weren't long enough to penetrate deep enough to do any real damage. Campbell was still sweating though as he opened on another one of the larger bat-like kaiju with *Ragnarok Valkyrie*'s cannons. The blast caught the bat thing at point-blank range as it swept in towards the mech's head with its clawed feet extended. Its guts and innards exploded from its mangled form as the cannons' rounds ripped its body into pieces.

"There are too many of them!" Geddy yelled over the comm as *Entropic Rush* started running out of the concentrated center of the kaiju swarm that swirled around the four mechs. The mech built speed as it went, batting kaiju that swooped in as it ran.

"Lieutenant Leigh! What the hell are you doing?" Major Leiber roared over the comm.

Geddy didn't answer her. Before Major Leiber could yell anything else, a trio of the kaiju flyers slammed into *Sand Stomper*. Their claws and teeth dug into the mech's armor as they clung to the hull of its upper body. The earlier damage to *Sand Stomper*'s right knee betrayed Major Leiber as she took a swing at them. Between the sudden movement and the weight of the kaiju flyers clinging to *Sand Stomper,* the knee blew out in an explosion of sparks and flame. Major Leiber screamed as *Sand Stomper* careened, totally unbalanced, to the left and then toppled onto the sand. One of the kaiju flyers on it was crushed beneath the mech's flailing arms. The other two managed to keep their claws in *Sand Stomper*. They tore frantically at the mech, trying to dig their way in to reach the human they knew was housed in its pilot compartment there.

"Major Leiber is down!" Campbell shouted over the comm. "*Sand Stomper* just dropped out of the comm. link!"

Campbell could see the giant bat-like creature tearing at *Sand Stomper*'s already heavily damaged leg with its claws. The other kaiju flyer, a strange reptilian thing with a beak, pecked at the mech's chest, ripping away pieces of the armor there with each strike. There was little he could do about it from *Ragnarok Valkyrie*'s current position. If he brought the mech's wrist cannons to bear on the kaiju flyers, he'd hit Major Leiber's mech in the process. Geddy in his mech *Entropic Rush* had ran out of the heart of the battle. Whatever Geddy was up to he hoped it was more than just making a mad dash for safety. That left Peter in *Hulking Diablo* to come to the major's aid. Unfortunately, Peter had his hands full at the moment. The bulk of the kaiju flyers were concentrating on *Hulking Diablo*. *Hulking Diablo* was swinging its axes like a berserker, hacking the kaiju circling it around it. Its right axe caught a kaiju flyer resembling a dragon on its back, the axe biting into the creature's spine and severing it despite not cutting all the way through its body. The blow knocked the kaiju down to land at the mech's feet. One of *Hulking Diablo*'s massive feet fell upon the kaiju's thrashing body and crushed it into the sand. *Hulking Diablo*'s other axe swept outward in a wide arc, slicing away parts of three other kaiju flyer's body as it went. One of them dropped from the air, its head gone from its neck, as the other two beat their wings frantically to escape another strike from the axe. The kaiju flyers were getting in their own blows against the mech, however. Entire patches of *Hulking Diablo*'s chest and shoulders were torn and jagged from where they claws had rent it. A good third of *Hulking Diablo*'s head was gone. Sparks flew from the exposed and damaged circuits there. For all its fury, *Hulking Diablo* was slowly being overwhelmed. Nearly a dozen kaiju flyer corpses lay scattered upon the sand taken out by its axes and the mech had wounded even more of the creatures, but it wasn't enough.

Kicking *Ragnarok Valkyrie* into motion, Campbell poured on the speed as the mech charged toward where *Sand Stomper* was fighting for its life. *Sand Stomper*'s hands had closed on the kaiju attacking its chest. They held the monster away so that its beak could no longer make contact with its barely intact chest. Campbell tried again to make contact with Major Leiber inside the mech but all that answered him over the comm link was static.

As he got closer, the kaiju at work on *Sand Stomper*'s damaged leg finally pulled it completely loose from the mech's body at the knee. Campbell angled *Ragnarok Valkyrie* just right to get a shot at the monster. *Ragnarok Valkyrie*'s wrist cannons blazed, hosing the beast with a stream of continuous fire that caused it to dance about wildly as they blasted through its body. The kaiju's mangled and blood-drenched body flopped to lie still on top of the leg it had just yanked off of *Sand Stomper*.

The eyes of the kaiju flyer that *Sand Stomper* was holding away from its chest went wide as it noticed *Ragnarok Valkyrie*'s presence and knew its life was over. It shrieked as Campbell maneuvered *Ragnarok Valkyrie* so that one of its wrist cannon was almost touching the side of the kaiju flyer's head and opened fire. The monster's brains sprayed out of the exit wound the bullets that struck it left in their wake. With the beast dead, *Sand Stomper* flung the thing's corpse away and then thudded fully onto its back again like an exhausted warrior who had no fight left in her.

****

Captain Merrick, at Major Leiber's command, had kept the hover tanks of his unit moving forward despite the kaiju attack. The beasts were focused on the mechs, and at any rate, the main guns of the hover tanks could only be elevated so far. Hover tanks were poor combatants when it came to engaging airborne foes. He had led the tanks outside the battle zone where the kaiju flyers and mechs were engaged before bringing them to a halt. Now though, he ordered them to come about. They were at a range which allowed them to better use their main guns against the beasts. Major Leiber hadn't specifically banned his hover tanks from entering the battle, and from the look of things, her mechs needed all the help they could get.

"All units, pick your targets and prepare to engage on my mark," Captain Merrick over the com-link. He knew he was taking a risk and not just in ticking off his C.O. If the kaiju flyers broke off from the mechs and came after them, his tanks would be little more than sitting ducks for the creatures. Hover tanks moved like lightning compared to their Old World counterparts, but against creatures like the kaiju flyers, they had no chance of outrunning or outmaneuvering them. If Major Leiber and her mechs failed to stop the monsters though, Captain Merrick and his tanks would be just as dead whether they attempted to turn the tide of the battle or not.

There were seventeen tanks under Captain Merrick's command, each with a crew of two to three aboard it. They all opened up at once as he shouted, "Fire at will!"

Three tanks, including his command tank, concentrated their fire on one of the larger bat-like kaiju flyers. The first explosion dug a gaping hole in the creature's side. The second marked the side of its face, blazing away at the hair and flesh there. The third missed the monster entirely as it flailed about from the pain inflicted by the first two. It swooped about in the air, diving onto a course that would bring it directly into the center of the tanks' ranks.

The other hover tanks had aimed for smaller targets. Their fire brought down four of the kaiju flyers with three confirmed kills. It was impossible to tell if the fourth flyer was merely wounded or dead as it came down on the other side of a distant hill from the tanks' position.

The barrage from the tanks didn't bring the fury of the kaiju flyers upon his unit as Captain Merrick feared it might. The beasts, except for the one large bat-like creature, all remained focused on tearing apart Major Leiber's mech units. Still, the lone, giant creature was more than enough of a threat as it landed amid the row of tanks and lashed out at them with its wings and the clawed hands at their ends. One tank was rolled over onto its side and then flung sideways into another from the powerful thrust of its fans as it tried vainly to right itself. It crashed into the other tank and both of them went up in flames, blossoming into an expanding cloud of fire and debris. The bat-like kaiju flopped downward, grabbing up a tank that had opened up on it with its top-mounted machine gun. The gunner died instantly, upper body crushed and smeared onto the tank's armor as the beast's hand closed around it. The bat-like kaiju flung the tank away like a toy. It went spiraling through the air to smash into the ground nearly a mile away, exploding on impact there.

"All units, break formation and concentrate your fire on this bastard! We've got to take her out before she takes us out!" Captain Merrick ordered.

The firing line of tanks broke up, each pushing its engines to the max in an effort to get clear of the giant bat-like kaiju that had landed among them. Tanks went howling away from the monster in all directions, most of them hammering the beast with their machine guns as they fled. Bullets ripped and tore at the bat-like kaiju's body, spotting its body with jagged holes as yellow blood leaked from the monster's wounds. For all the visible gore, the machine gun fire did little more than anger the creature more than it already was. One of its clawed hands slashed downwards at one of the fleeing hover tanks. The claws parted the tank's armor like a razor cutting through paper. The tank's topside gunner and machine gun were shredded even as the blow sent the tank half-rolling, half-bouncing across the sand. Captain Merrick watched another icon representing one of the tanks under his command wink out on his tactical display as it did so. His command tank currently had its rear towards the monster and his driver had the pedal to the metal.

"Bring us around!" Captain Merrick ordered his driver. "And take us straight down that monster's throat!"

"Sir?" the driver cried even as she moved to follow his order.

"Gunner, aim for that demon thing's head and take it clean off its shoulder!" Captain Merrick yelled.

The bat-like kaiju turned to snarl at Captain Merrick's command tank as it came flying towards it. It raised one of its clawed hands to deliver a blow that surely would have ended the command tank had not Captain Merrick shouted, "Fire!"

The command tank's main gun flashed at the kaiju lowering head as it moved in to strike, the shot smacking into its skull at near point-blank range. The beast's brain splattered out of the back side of its head as the heavy round punctured bone then brain matter then bone again. The bat-like kaiju's body snapped upwards, a hole clean through its forehead, and stood at full height for a fraction of a second as if the beast's system needed that time to realize it was dead.

"Evasive maneuvers!" Captain Merrick screamed as the thing's massive corpse toppled falling straight over the command tank's position. The command tank's driver jerked the heavy vehicle hard to the left as the tank's engine whined, pressed to its limits. The tank cleared the area where the bat-like kaiju's body flopped onto the sand by a hair's breath. The shockwave from the impact of the creature's weight striking the sand behind could be held inside the hover tank even though it wasn't touching the ground. The air disturbance was enough to shake it and leave the driver cursing as the command tank was shoved hard to the right. Captain Merrick was terrified the driver was going to lose control but she didn't. The tank zigged and zagged wildly but she fought it onto a straight course that leveled out its fans. Captain Merrick let out a sigh of relief as the tank stabilized.

The rest of his scattered unit had gotten clear of the bat-like kaiju and came to stop awaiting further orders. The loss of three tanks so quickly kept him from ordering them to engage the kaiju again. Instead, he ordered them to hold position and waited to see if Major Leiber and her mechs could pull off a miracle against the number of kaiju the mechs were facing.

****

Sand Stomper lay on the ground, one of its legs gone and its chest pecked and clawed into a mass of ravaged metal. It was clear that the mech wouldn't be getting up anytime soon. Campbell, piloting *Ragnarok Valkyrie*, kept guard over it. *Sand Stomper*'s comms were offline so Major Leiber couldn't order him not to do so. Major Leiber might have to make hard calls and leave people at the mercy of the enemy but Campbell wasn't in command. He had no such restraints upon his actions in terms of deciding who lived and who died. The hover tanks appeared to be out of harm's way and the other two mechs were operational and able to handle themselves; even if *Hulking Diablo* looked on the verge of falling, it was still in the fight. If anyone could take on a swarm of kaiju flyers by himself, Peter was the pilot to do it. Campbell had faith in the man's love of bloodshed to get him through. As to Geddy, well, where in the devil he had ran off to was anyone's guess, but he and *Entropic Rush* weren't in danger. Major Leiber and *Sand Stomper* though were completely defenseless without him.

A trio of kaiju flyers came flying at *Ragnarok Valkyrie* and *Sand Stomper*. It was clear they wanted at *Sand Stomper* more than wanted to head to head with Campbell's fully functional *Ragnarok Valkyrie*. They angled their flight in an attempt to get around him but Campbell was ready for them. He fired a burst of rounds that clipped one of the kaiju's wings and sent it spiraling headfirst into the sand with the crunching sound of breaking skull bone and punctured the guts of another. The gutted kaiju tried to pull up and come about to make a run for it with its intestines leaking from what was once its stomach but the strands of its intestines wrapped around one of the creature's wings, entangling it. The kaiju flipped in the air and fell from the sky to go bouncing across the sand out of Campbell's line of sight. The third and oddest looking of the three kaiju made it past him, however. It landed with a thud on *Sand Stomper*'s ravaged chest. The thing's head was more insectoid than bird or reptile in nature and its speed was incredible. Even as Campbell twisted around the upper half *Ragnarok Valkyrie*'s body to get a shot at it, a long, tongue shot from its snout-like mouth with the speed of a striking serpent. The end of the tongue was hardened, much like a spear tip. It pierced *Sand Stomper*'s head and pilot compartment, apparently hitting something vital there because the mech's head exploded in a shower of spewing flames and erupting metal fragments.

"No!" Campbell wailed but it was too late. The damage was done. Major Leiber was dead. *Ragnarok Valkyrie* stumbled a step as Campbell's mind reeled in disbelief at what had just happened.

Campbell's attention was torn away from the horrific sight of the fires burning and raging inside of what remained of *Sand Stomper*'s head by Peter's voice over the comm.

"Can I get a little help here, guys?" Peter shouted.

On his tactical view screen, Campbell saw that nearly a dozen of the smaller kaiju flyers had attached themselves to *Hulking Diablo*'s armored body. They clung to it, tearing away at it with their claws and teeth even as the giant mech continued to swing its axes at the larger members of the swarm.

Campbell disengaged *Ragnarok Valkyrie*'s wrist cannons. He hated to it but he needed a close-in weapon more at the moment. Small charges activated, exploding, to pop the mounted cannons free of *Ragnarok Valkyrie*'s wrists. Beneath where they had rested, the armor separated, sliding open as Campbell flung the mech's arms forward. Two, long chains were flung from the openings. As the chains extended, their tips condensed, wrapping over themselves to form mace-like heads. As they did so, a feral grin parted Campbell's lips. It was time for the battle to truly get up close and personal.

"The major's dead!" Campbell shouted over the comm. as *Ragnarok Valkyrie*'s legs pumped beneath it and the mech charged forward to come to *Hulking Diablo*'s aid. Campbell heard Peter give an unemotional grunt of acknowledgement to what he had said. He couldn't tell if Peter really didn't give a crap or was just too busy with the kaiju to say anything more.

Ragnarok Valkyrie swung one of its maces into the swarm of the kaiju, knocking several of them from the sky as the weapon shattered their bones. Campbell then swung the mech's other chain upwards to ensnare one the last of the larger bat-like kaiju. The chain crushed bone where it wrapped around the monster before, and with a jerk, *Ragnarok Valkyrie* yanked the monster from the sky, slamming it into the sand of the Waste.

"Not bad," he heard Peter comment over the comm. "Not bad at all, Campbell."

"Get clear of the kaiju!" Geddy called to them suddenly.

"Where the hell have you ...?" Peter started but Geddy cut him off.

"Now!" Geddy screamed, the urgency of his tone was as sharp as Peter and Campbell's surprise to hear from him.

Peter threw *Hulking Diablo* forward and flat onto the sand like a man trying to dodge a bullet as *Ragnarok Valkyrie* leaped sideways.

A screeching wall of sonic energy plowed through the kaiju swarm, decimating it in a single blast. The handful of kaiju that survived soared upwards and away from the three mechs as *Entropic Rush* bounded across the sand to stand where *Hulking Diablo* and *Ragnarok Valkyrie* had been.

"Holy mother of goodness!" Peter exclaimed. "What in the devil did you just do?"

Campbell was too shocked to say anything. He just stared at the image of *Entropic Rush* on his tactical viewer in awe.

"That's a like move I like to call Sonic Blitz, gentlemen," Geddy laughed. "It takes a while to power up though. Sorry about that."

"Man, you wasted those bastards." Peter was cackling inside *Hulking Diablo* as the heavy mech rose to its feet.

"Good thing too," Geddy said. "That just took everything but *Entropic Rush*'s emergency backup power. I'm running on close to empty, guys."

"I don't think those kaiju will be coming back anytime soon," Campbell commented. "What's left of them, I mean."

A moment of awkward silence ticked by before Geddy said, "Did I just hear you say that Major Leiber is dead?"

"Take a look for yourself," Campbell gestured at the flaming ruins of *Sand Stomper*'s headless form where it lay in the sand with one of *Ragnarok Valkyrie*'s hands.

"Dang," Geddy breathed slowly, stretching out the word. "So that leaves you in command, doesn't it?"

"No," Campbell answered. "Captain Merrick is the ranking officer now."

"What?" Peter roared. "That's whacked. I'm not taking orders from some tank commander."

"He's a captain actually," Geddy chimed in.

"Doesn't matter, Peter," Campbell said flatly. "He's in charge."

"Surprised he hasn't tapped into our comm. network yet," Geddy said.

"I have Lieutenant Leigh," Captain Merrick's voice took them all by surprise. "Major Leiber may be dead but our mission isn't over."

"No it's not," Peter growled. There was a long pause before he added, "Sir."

"Look, Lieutenant Keene, I know you mech boys aren't used to be bossed around by someone who isn't another pilot. I don't like it either, but it's how the cards have fallen. Don't give me any crap and I won't give you any either. Understood?" Captain Merrick said.

"Understood," Peter answered grudgingly.

"So what's the plan, sir?" Geddy asked.

"Right now, we're gonna reach out to the support units we left at Canton and allow them time to catch up to us. Pressing on as we are would be madness." Captain Merrick seemed to wait for Peter to challenge him, but to even Campbell's surprise, Peter didn't.

"Stay alert in the meantime," Captain Merrick ordered and then ended his transmission.

****

"Major Leiber is confirmed dead, sir," Major Steiner informed Colonel Jaeger.

Colonel Jaeger frowned as he sat in the command chair of the war room. There were several techs in the room aside from the two them. The techs each manned their own comm./satellite/drone stations, keeping an eye on the developing situation with the two taskforces in route to the Greenery's capital. Taskforce Alpha was nearing its final stopping position before reaching the capital. Aside from a few almost guerilla-style attacks, it had encountered very little resistance. Instead, the Greenery forces that could have truly engaged it had merely continued to pull back out of its path. Taskforce Beta on the other hand had suffered severe losses. It had been assigned to dealing with the Greenery city of Canton, and while it had destroyed the city, that battle and the engagement with a swarm of kaiju that followed it had taken its toll on the unit. Colonel Jaeger wasn't overly concerned with the losses in regards to the lesser units of the taskforce, but the loss of *Sand Stomper* and Major Leiber was a powerful blow to his plans by the enemy. Mechs weren't cheap or easy to build. Each took months and a great deal of resources. They couldn't be replaced as quickly as the Greenery's kaiju could even before the new rumors that the Greenery had discovered a real means of mass-producing giant kaiju on a level that could likely mean the end of the long war and of Steel Heart itself.

As if the loss of *Sand Stomper* wasn't bad enough, the loss of Major Leiber, Taskforce Beta's commanding officer, was an even harsher blow. He had handpicked her to lead the assault on the Greenery's capital. With her gone, that left a young tank captain named Merrick in command of her half of the overall assault force and Major Rowley in command of the overall force. Rowley was even younger and more inexperienced than Captain Merrick was in a sense. Rowley had joined up straight out of Steel Heart's academy and worked his way up the ranks inside the safety of the capital itself. Before being assigned to accompany Major Leiber as her support, the young major had led only a few defense skirmishes along the now-shattered front lines. There was no way in hell that Colonel Jaeger was going to leave the major in charge of the overall assault on the Greenery. There was too much at stake. Handing over full command to Captain Merrick was an equally bad idea. Mech pilots looked down, no pun intended, on tankers and truthfully a lot of tankers were troopers who didn't have what it took to pilot a mech. Having given Captain Merrick's file a quick read through in the last half hour, Colonel Jaeger knew the man was a competent and seasoned officer but that didn't mean the man had what it took to lead an assault of the scale as the attack on the Greenery's capital. Even if he did, would the mech pilots in the field listen to a mere tanker? What kind of effect would Captain Merrick being placed in overall command have on their morale? Colonel Jaeger needed someone that he could be sure the other mech pilots would get behind and obey. Captain Merrick just wasn't that.

Colonel Jaeger had ordered a team of field techs to find a way inside the wreckage of *Sand Stomper* in the vain hope that somehow Major Leiber had survived. With her death now confirmed, he was going to have to make a very hard choice. He could call off the assault on the capital, that was true, but doing so if the rumors of the new method of Greenery kaiju production were more than rumors was too dangerous a gamble to take as he saw things. That meant his only real option was to get someone out there who could lead the assault that he trusted to be able to handle the job.

He noticed Major Steiner watching him closely.

"What is it, Steiner?" he asked.

"A word in private, sir?" Major Steiner asked.

Colonel Jaeger nodded getting up from his command seat. "Captain Reed." He nodded at the chair he had just vacated. "If you would until I return."

"Yes, sir!" Captain Reed barked and took over.

With Major Steiner on his heels, the two of them stepped out of the war room and into the empty hallway beyond it.

"Now what is it, Major?" Colonel Jaeger demanded.

"I was thinking we need to send a new C.O. to head up the assault on the Greenery, sir," Major Steiner told him.

"And how exactly do we do that, Major?" Colonel Jaeger growled. "We have very few aircraft at our disposal and that's what it would take to get someone new there in time. Besides, that swarm of kaiju flyers that hammered Taskforce Beta may not be the only one of its kind out there."

Major Steiner looked nervous as he answered, "Samurai One, sir. She's your answer."

Colonel Jaeger flinched at the mention of the mech's name. He had to hold himself back from springing forward and slapping a hand over the young major's mouth.

"Not another word, Major," Colonel Jaeger warned. "Not here anyway."

"I understand that we haven't had a chance to tell the Council of Engineers about her yet sir but …" Major Steiner stammered.

"Enough!" Colonel Jaeger snapped. Major Steiner took a step back, his face turning pale.

Colonel Jaeger forced himself to calm down. "As it so happens, Major, I agree with you, but you need to keep your mouth shut. Do I make myself clear?"

"Yes, sir." Major Steiner nodded.

Taking an archaic notepad from the pocket of his uniform, he scrawled his orders on it, tearing them off, and handed them to the young major.

"Take these and follow them to the letter," Colonel Jaeger told him sternly. "And if you utter another word about any of this before I tell you to, I'll shoot you myself. You won't have to for the court martial that will likely be waiting for us both when all this over with."

He watched Major Steiner read over the orders, the young major's expression lighting up as he did so. "Understood, sir." Major Steiner beamed at him and then turned and ran down the corridor in the direction of the colonel's office.

When Major Steiner had disappeared from sight, Colonel Jaeger sighed, heading back into the war room.

****

Worm woke up Joster at the crack of dawn. The two of them had downed a quick breakfast of kaiju meat and water then gotten moving southward. The heat of the sun baked them as they trudged over the sand. Worm hadn't agreed to help him get home but they were heading south in the general direction of the

Greenery capital, and for that, Joster was grateful. The old man really knew his way around the Waste. Worm used his spear like a walking stick as they worked their way up a small dune. Joster still carried the tech revolver he had looted from an abandoned jeep he had stumbled onto. There was only one bullet remaining in the weapon but Joster held on to it anyway, keeping the pistol tucked under the front of his belt. Sometimes a single bullet could be enough to save your life. In his hands, he carried a new weapon that Worm had given him from the pack he carried. It was a small, machine gun-like weapon that the old man said was called an UZI. Worm had warned him that the weapon didn't have much stopping power against a wild kaiju but that its rate of fire was impressive. It might not stop a wild kaiju outright without some massive good luck, but it sure would mess one up if its magazine was emptied into one of the creatures.

The old man's kindness was shocking to Joster. For a person who looked and acted rough enough that Joster had actually believed the old man might consider eating him, Worm was proving to be a better traveling companion than even another soldier from the Greenery would likely have been. He just couldn't figure the old nomad out. Worm's thoughts on his people and those of Steel Heart were detestable at best according to the ideology that Joster had been raised in. The old nomad viewed both sides as equal evils. He couldn't see the beauty of the Greenery's path or the sheer horror of Steel Heart's. How Worm couldn't understand that the techs of Steel Heart wanted to rape the world of its resources and pollute it even more than its current state was a mystery to him.

"Hold up, boy," Worm whispered as they neared the top of the dune they were about to crest. "Listen."

The wind had been howling the better part of the morning. Joster had been afraid that it would kick up a sandstorm from the level of its fury, but the old man had assured him it wasn't to that point yet and they were fine for the time being. Joster stopped where he was and strained his ears in an attempt to hear what the old nomad was hearing. It took a moment but he finally did. Coming from somewhere distant on the other side of the dune was the sound of something akin to heavy machinery at work.

"What the ...?" Joster started but Worm leaped at him, covering his mouth as the old man took the two of them down onto the sand.

Worm gestured for Joster to keep his mouth shut and slowly crawled up to the top of the dune, taking a careful peek over it. Joster snaked his way up after the old man. It was all he could do not to scream as he poked his head up just enough to get a look over the top of the dune.

In the distance, he saw what looked to be an entire taskforce worth of Steel Heart hover tanks and mechs accompanied by support vehicles. Steel Heart infantry and repair personnel scurried about beneath the towering forms of four giant mechs. All of the techs were busy. It looked like they were making the final preparations to head into the battle of their lives.

"Your Greenery's capital ain't that far from here, boy," Worm told him. "I reckon that's where they're heading."

Joster was torn between whether telling the old nomad that the two of them needed to run for their lives or demanding that Worm help him find a way to stop the Tech forces before they got moving again. He knew the second bit was insane but his sense of duty tossed it into his mind anyway. The two of them wouldn't last half a second against the Tech forces they were looking at.

In the end, he opted to let the old nomad plot their course of action, asking, "What should we do?"

"We keep our heads to the sand and wait for them to move out," Worm said, staring at him as if he was insane. "What else can we do?"

Joster gave a half-hearted shrug, not willing to admit he had actually considered trying to go up against the techs even for a brief second. "I don't know … something. I guess I just figured you might have some kind of a plan for dealing with stuff like this."

"The Steel Heart folks have rarely ever been this deep into your people's territory before, kid. That's the largest group of them I have ever seen," Worm said, frowning. "Right now, we need to shuffle back down this dune as slowly and carefully as we can and pray hard they don't notice we're here. Some of those mechs have sensors like you wouldn't believe."

"Halt where you are!" a booming voice rang out over the howling of the wind from behind them. Joster and Worm rolled over to see a smaller, Wolf-class mech standing over them. The pilot's voice had been amplified by the system of the mech. The barrel of the heavy, belt-fed weapon it carried was aimed directly at them.

Worm let his spear drop from his grasp and slowly raised both hands above his head. Joster followed his example, tossing aside his UZI.

****

Grand Duala Minerva was pleased. The kaiju eggs had hatched. Of the close to four dozen eggs, thirty-eight new true kaiju had been born and were growing into adulthood at a staggering rate. Never in the history of the Greenery's hatchery had so many been spawned in a single hatching. These weren't merely flyers or the lesser kaiju that were used as infantry and cannon fodder. No, they were each a great beast that would become a primary weapon of the Greenery's forces. Thanks to the growth acceleration process overseen by Mother Gretch and the rest of the Kaiju Mothers, by tomorrow, these true kaiju would be ready to let loose upon the invading Steel Heart army that even now continued its push towards the capital.

Duala Mate Denkirch approached her where she sat upon the floor of her chambers, crossed-legged, palms resting on her knees. She could sense the elation flowing through him.

"Grand Duala." He smiled at her, taking a seat on the floor in front of her. "I have just linked with the survivors of one of our flyer swarms that engaged one of the main groups of Tech forces in route to us."

There was no need for the two of them to use words. Both of them were powerful psychics, but after the stern warnings she had given Denkirch about forgetting his place, he kept his thoughts, beyond those he spoke aloud, to himself. She didn't blame him for doing so. In his place, she would have done the same.

"And?" Grand Duala Minerva pressed him.

"Our flyers confirm that there are only eight mechs among the forces bearing down on us and one of those was destroyed when that just returned engaged half their number to the northwest." Denkirch grinned.

Grand Duala Minerva's laughter boomed out of her and echoed off the stone walls of her chambers. "Seven," she cackled. "A mere seven mechs!"

"Indeed." Denkirch nodded. "Steel Heart rolled the dice that they could stop us before our latest batch of true kaiju were ready and lost. Their invasion force will be slaughtered upon reaching us and then …"

"Then it will be our turn to bring horror to their doorstep," Grand Duala Minerva finished for him.

"All the evidence points to the invasion forces being the bulk of what they have, Grand Duala. They can't have more than a handful of mechs held in reserve," Duala Mate Denkirch said.

"We've seen very few of their smaller mechs," Grand Duala Minerva pointed out.

"True but that doesn't matter," Duala Mate Denkirch told her. "Those things aren't much better than their hover tanks against true kaiju. Even if they held back five dozen of those 'Wolves,' as I believe the Techs call them, it won't be enough. Our kaiju will tear through their ranks easily. We have sprung the perfect trap and Steel Heart will fall to us at last."

"Overconfidence suits you well, Denkirch," Grand Duala Minerva stared at him.

Duala Mate Denkirch blinked. "Overconfidence? How can you say that? With the numbers we'll have at our disposal by the time the Techs arrive, there can be no question of the outcome ahead of us."

"How old are you, Denkirch?" Grand Duala Minerva asked him frankly though she already knew the answer.

"I was born of the Vats …" he began but she cut him off.

"Not long enough ago it seems," she repeated the words. "You are so very young, Denkirch. You've no lack of power or intellect but wisdom is still beyond your grasp."

Denkirch's eyes flashed with anger but he held his tongue.

"I have lived long enough to see the evil that infests the people of Steel Heart endure and prevail against us many times before even when our final victory appeared to be at hand and no hope was left to those fools. Do not underestimate them, Denkirch. For all their ignorance and pride, they are a formidable people," Grand Duala Minerva frowned. "Let's not celebrate our final victory until it has been achieved. To do so at this point would be nothing more than folly on our part."

"But, Grand Duala …" Denkirch began to argue with her.

"Enough, Denkirch," she cautioned him. "Go now and ready our new kaiju for the coming dawn. Our enemies will soon be here and you must be fully prepared to face them. The new kaiju will still be young and it will be up to you to control them. I must my save my strength for what will come after should you succeed."

"I will not fail, Grand Duala," Denkirch said so forcefully that he reminded her of a male ape pounding upon its chest. "Of that, I assure you."

Grand Duala Minerva watched him rise and leave her chambers. When he was gone, she found her center once more, closing her eyes, and reached out with her mind to commune with the secrets of the future. Her mother had been a pre-cog of the highest order. Grand Duala Minerva's psi-talents lay along another path, but from time to time, like this evening, she still tried to emulate her mother's talent. Though victory seemed assured when one looked at things in a logical manner, something troubled her about what lay ahead, something she couldn't quite put her finger on. It was nothing more than a feeling really but it clawed at her, warning that not all the cards upon the table had been revealed as yet, and she longed to know what those unrevealed cards might be.

****

The Wolf-class mech stood fifteen feet tall. Its sand-colored armor gleamed in the harsh rays of the sun. The mech was human shaped and carried a nasty-looking, heavy, belt-fed weapon. Joster had seen such mechs many times before but never had he been so close to one. It felt as if he were staring up at a giant. The mech was small in comparison to the kaiju-killer mechs of the Tech forces, but this close, it seemed far more massive than it truly was to Joster.

Both he and Worm had discarded their weapons. Joster wanted to fight but he knew that if the old nomad had opted to toss aside his weapons instead of making a go at taking out the lone mech facing them and making a run for it that he would have been dead if he had tried.

"Both of you, on your knees," the mech pilot ordered them. "Hands behind your heads."

Worm did as he was told, leaving Joster no choice but to do the same.

"We mean you no harm," Worm told the pilot in the mech. "I'm nothing more than a nomad trying to survive out here."

"Sure thing, old man," the mech pilot growled in a disgusted tone. "And your friend is wearing a Greenery military uniform because he found it here in the Waste, right?"

"As a matter of fact." Worm smirked.

"Don't get smart with me, old man," the mech pilot warned. Apparently, he had called in their position to the main body of the Tech force nearby because a group of five Tech infantry troops appeared over the top of the dune and made their way down to where they were. Two of the infantry troopers set about collecting their discarded weapons while two others approached them, guns at the ready, and begin to do one-handed frisks of their bodies.

"Hey now!" Worm shouted. "I'm a free man. I have rights!"

The infantry troops snickered as the pilot in the mech said, "You're not a citizen of Steel Heart, old man. You're living deep in Greenery territory with one of the freaks' soldiers as your traveling companion. Whatever rights you think you had, you forfeited them the second you allowed him to join up with you."

"Sir! They're carrying a grenade," one of the infantry troopers shouted, taking the weapon, and lifting it for the mech pilot to see.

"Give me one good reason why I shouldn't just kill the two of you here and now and be done with it," the mech pilot said.

Joster saw Worm glance at him with a sorrowful expression.

"You're right. That one there is a Greenery soldier. I found him wandering the Waste after a battle that destroyed the unit he was assigned to," Worm confessed. "Don't you think it might be useful to see what kind of information you can get out of him?"

"Name and rank, soldier," the mech pilot ordered Joster.

"My name is Joster," he answered. "We don't really have the same sort of rank structure that you do, but I'm a warrior if that means anything to you."

The pilot inside the mech and the infantry troopers all burst into laughter.

"And a mighty one at that," one of them taunted him.

"Lost in the Waste and saved by an old man," another snorted. "That's a feat to be sung about for the ages right there that is."

"Well, Warrior Joster," the mech pilot laughed, his tone a mocking one, "today is your lucky day. My C.O. actually wants you alive."

"And what about me?" Worm demanded. "I brought him to you, didn't I?"

"Sorry, old man," the mech pilot said, "your luck has just run out."

In a very calm and fluid motion, one of the Tech infantry troopers snapped his rifle up at Worm. Before the old man could even try to argue more, the trooper squeezed the weapon's trigger. A five-round burst of high-powered rounds ripped into Worm's chest, splattering the sand with his blood and pieces of his shattered ribs. Worm's body was flung backwards by the impact of the rounds and toppled onto the sand, rolling down the dune to rest at the mech's feet.

"By all that's holy!" Joster shouted. "You didn't have to kill him! He was just an old nomad like he said he was."

"Not your call to make, green boy," the mech pilot snarled. "Now settle down or I'll do the same to you."

Joster stared at the head of the Wolf-class mech where the upper body of its pilot surely rested with hatred burning in his eyes but he kept his mouth shut. He didn't resist as the Tech infantry troopers shoved him ahead of them, walking him towards the Techs' main force on the other side of the dune.

Terrified and in awe of what he saw as they led him over the dune, Joster promised himself he would die with dignity. The Wolf-class mech stomped along behind him and the infantry troopers. He realized again just how small it was he looked up the four real giants that watched over the Techs' forces.

A man dressed in the uniform of a Steel Heart major came forward to meet them. Two more Wolf-class mechs walked at his side as escorts. The major and the two mechs stopped several yards short of where the infantry troopers brought Joster to a stop at.

"I am Major Nathan Rowley in command of Taskforce Alpha," the major told him. "I am told you are a warrior of the Greenery and the uniform you wear seems to confirm that fact."

Joster said nothing. He didn't know what to say. He fantasized about grabbing a rifle from the hands of one of the Tech infantry troopers behind him and gunning the major down where he stood. His rational mind kept him from doing so though. Even if he was able to yank a weapon from one of the Tech infantry, the mechs that stood protecting the major would blow him to pieces before he could use it.

"I have very little time," Major Rowley told him. "If you wish to live, there are things I would like to know. Do you understand me?"

"You're offering me my freedom if I tell you … what?" Joster asked, trying to keep his voice from showing just how terrified and angry he felt.

"I want to know everything that you do about your capital and what's waiting for us there," Major Rowley answered. "If you can provide use with something that I deem useful, then yes, I'll let you go. You're no threat to us out here and your capital will be in flames regardless before you could ever hope to reach it."

****

Colonel Jaeger had relieved Captain Reed and taken command of the Steel Heart's war room again some time ago. He sat in his chair, listening to the incoming reports from Taskforce Beta as it scrambled to join up with Taskforce Alpha for the final push of the invasion into the Greenery lands. Everything, other than having a C.O. on site that he trusted, appeared to be going as well as he could hope for.

"Colonel!" one the war room's techs, he thought was named Berrong, shouted at him from her station. "I've got a power surge, sir!"

The other techs in the war room turned to look at her as if she had lost her mind.

"Which Taskforce?" her direct supervisor, a senior tech named Harold, snapped at her.

"No, sir," Colonel Jaeger heard her answer. "It's not coming from either Taskforce. It's coming from inside this city."

"That's impossible!" Senior Tech Harold shouted and left his station, heading toward her.

"Stand down, Harold," Colonel Jaeger ordered his voice calm and smooth.

Harold shot him an angry glare before realizing what he had done. The anger vanished from the senior tech's eyes, replaced by fear. "Yes, sir," Harold said and returned to his own station.

"Where is this power surge you're detecting coming from exactly?" Colonel Jaeger asked the female tech.

"From Councilor Sheehan's factory, sir," she answered with a confused expression. "It's a mech power signature, sir. I would stake my life on it. But it's not like any I have ever seen."

"Shelia!" Harold shouted at her. "Double check your readings!"

"I have, sir; triple checked them even. It's real, sir." She held her ground, no matter how crazy she sounded. Everyone in the war room knew that Steel Heart only had ten, now nine, functioning mechs registered and operational. Seven were in the field, assigned to the taskforces closing in on the Greenery's capital and the other two were tucked away in their construction pits as a reserve should the Greenery somehow opt to make a move against the city in reprisal.

Colonel Jaeger rubbed at his cheeks with the tips of the fingers of his right hand. "*I* never said I doubted you, Specialist Berrong. Tell me more about why this signature is so different."

"It's two-point-five times that of a normal class-seven mech, sir," she answered. "The energy output of the thing is unbelievable."

"I see." Colonel Jaeger feigned a frown. "It seems Councilor Sheehan has been hiding something from us all, eh?"

"With all due respect, that's a pretty big accusation to make sir," Senior Tech Harold challenged him. "Surely it's just a glitch of some kind in Specialist Berrong's station."

Captain Reed, who had kept quiet until now, spoke up. "If it's not though, Councilor Sheehan is guilty of outright treason," he reminded them all.

"Agreed." Colonel Jaeger nodded. "Ready my transport. I'm going to investigate this matter personally. Captain Merrick, you have command until I return."

Captain Reed gave him a hard nod and moved to take over the command chair as Colonel Jaeger vacated it.

As Colonel Jaeger stepped out of the war room and an escort of four heavily armed guards met him, he allowed himself a slight smile. The four guardsmen were men he knew well. Major Steiner appeared to be following the orders Jaeger had given him to the letter.

The guardsmen accompanied him to the landing platform where the APC-like hover car he had requested was waiting. They followed him onto it, strapping into their seats as he headed up front to join the car's pilot.

"Get us there as quickly as you can, soldier," Colonel Jaeger said, easing into the empty copilot seat.

"Yes, sir," the pilot barked. The hover car lifted off, streaking across the sky above Steel Heart in route to Councilor Sheehan's factory.

Colonel Jaeger let out a sigh of relief as the hover car touched down outside of the factory and he saw both Major Steiner and the councilor waiting on him instead of a squad of

Intel Police. As soon as he was out of the car, Major Steiner ran over to him.

"She's prepped and ready, sir," the younger man told him. "All she needs is you."

The two of them clasped hands as if they were saying a final farewell and very likely they were.

"Good luck to you, Major," Colonel Jaeger said. "I hope to see you alive and well when I return."

"I hope so too." Major Steiner nodded.

"This way, Colonel," Councilor Sheehan urged him, leading him towards a section of the factory's exterior wall next to its proper entrance. "I rigged this up just for you." The councilor grinned. "It'll take you straight to where you need to go."

"Thank you … For everything," Colonel Jaeger said sincerely. "Whether it knows it or not, Steel Heart is in your debt."

"You just win this war, Colonel," Councilor Sheehan said. "You do that and anything else that happens from here on in will be worth it."

Councilor Sheehan waved a hand over the surface of the wall next to the door and a small section of it opened, a control panel sliding outward from it as a second doorway also opened next to the main entrance.

Colonel Jaeger stepped into it and closed behind him. There was a sudden lurch as the floor seemed to give way beneath him. He was inside a lift and it had just started moving. As the lift fell downwards, it reshaped itself about him. He gasped as he realized it was becoming the pilot compartment of a mech. The lift came to a halt, its impact against whatever it had landed on leaving his guts churning. As he sat in the pilot compartment that the lift had become, he could see system lights turning on all around him. A tactical display flickered into being in front where he sat. Samurai One was fully activated and ready for action. He wasted no time plugging into her through the cybernetic implants embedded in his body from his mech pilot days. Power like he had never known or even imagined could exist flowed through him. He had studied the schematics of the mech that the councilor had provide him with it but being tapped into Samurai One was something else altogether. He could feel every inch of her in his mind as he mentally reached out to run a pre-flight systems check. All systems were green. He hoped Major Steiner and the others had cleared out of the way above him because it was time to take Samurai One into the air where she belonged.

The thrusters on her back and feet roared to life as she began to rise from her concealed construction pit. She exploded through its roof and flew straight upwards into the clouds like a giant rocket, her arms flat against the sides of her body. Once she was clear of Councilor Sheehan's factory and well into the air, Colonel Jaeger leveled her out, extending her arms ahead of her in a fashion similar to superheroes in the pages of comics from the Old World. He set a course towards the Greenery capital and was gone before any of Steel Heart's defenses were able to engage him. He, Major Steiner, and Councilor Sheehan had pulled off their desperate plan and taken the entire city by completely by surprise. That surprise compounded with the sheer disbelief that the city's defensive forces had to have experienced at the sight of an unregistered mech taking flight had spared him from having to fight his way out of the city, and that was something he would be forever grateful for.

****

With the repairs as complete as they could be in the field and all the units of Taskforce Beta re-equipped and reloaded, Captain Merrick got them moving again. This time, the support vehicles accompanied the hover tanks and three remaining mechs that was the Taskforce's core. It didn't take them long to meet up with Taskforce Alpha. Campbell was interested to see how Captain Merrick was going to handle Major Rowley. Peter and Geddy were placing bets over the mechs' comlink as to who would end up in overall command.

As Taskforce Alpha came into sight, its four mechs joined their com-link, the two groups merging into a single fighting force. *Nuke Fist, Boomerang Charge, Steadfast Warrior,* and *Four-Arm Fury* were a welcome sight. All four of them looked pristine compared to *Ragnarok Valkyrie, Hulking Diablo,* and *Entropic Rush.* Of course, they hadn't been tasked with taking out a major Greenery city on their path to the capital or gone head to head with a swarm of kaiju flyers.

Captain Mitch, piloting *Steadfast Warrior,* took direct command of the mechs. Peter was already bragging to Duvall, in *Nuke Fist,* and Dundee, in *Boomerang Charge,* about the number of kills he had raked up in the battle with the swarm. Duvall argued that the swarm kills weren't kills of true kaiju and that they didn't count but Peter was standing his ground that at the very least the giant bat-like flyers counted as a true kaiju given their size and toughness. Lillian, in *Four-Arm Fury,* traded witty banter back and forth with Geddy. Campbell knew the lady to be as crazy as Peter was when it came to combat but she and Geddy had a "thing." The very existence of their relationship proved that opposites did attract. Geddy was a thin, little guy. His interests lay in music, books, and art. To say he was a geek was an understatement. The term nerd fitted him better. He was also a supremely talented engineer when it came to designing weapon systems for Steel Heart's mechs. It was his idea to create a multi-armed mech, and after proving the combat effectiveness of such a design, he had everyone behind getting *Four-Arm Fury* commissioned by his home factory. The two of them had met for the first time as the factory's head had put Geddy in charge of finding a pilot with the disjointed mental state needed to use four arms at once. For Lillian, the attraction between them had started right then and there. Geddy's natural aloofness had kept him from realizing how she felt until Campbell had stepped in. Once Campbell got Geddy's head out of the clouds long enough to see how Lillian felt, well, the rest was history. Campbell always had to stifle a laugh at the sight of the two of them together. Lillian was a good foot taller than Geddy and well-toned muscle from head to toe. She looked like she could pick up and break the little guy in half if he ever did anything that royally ticked her off. Campbell doubted that would ever happen though. Geddy was head over heels for Lillian and she was as much his world as the art and numbers he had loved above all else until he met her.

The four mechs of Taskforce Alpha shifted their position so that *Ragnarok Valkyrie, Hulking Diablo,* and *Entropic Rush* could join the defensive formation they had set up around the lesser units of the two taskforces or Battlegroup Alpha as they were now called. In addition to the seven mechs, Battlegroup

Alpha was composed for twenty-three hover tanks, a squad of six Wolf-class mechs, a battalion's worth of infantry troopers, and its accompanying support vehicles. Taskforce Alpha had taken some losses on its journey too but none as severe as what Taskforce Beta had. Whether or not their combined strength was really enough to take the heart of the Greenery was debatable as Campbell saw things, but they had all came too far to turn back at this point. Their success or failure depended entirely on just what was waiting for them inside the walls of the Greenery's capital. Campbell knew that aside from the kaiju swarm, neither taskforce had encountered any real resistance beyond limited guerilla attack. That meant either the Greenery was hurting even more than Colonel Jaeger claimed or their powers that be had called everything they had to the capital to defend it in one winner take all battle.

Campbell was surprised when Captain Merrick's voice suddenly came over the comlink shared by Battlegroup Alpha's seven mechs. At first, he assumed that the captain had ended up in charge of the Battlegroup and Geddy had won the bet he and Peter had made. He soon found out that wasn't the case, however.

"Colonel Jaeger is in route to our position," Captain Merrick said. "He'll be taking personal command of the assault on the Greenery's capital. We'll be holding here until either he arrives or he gives an order for us to do otherwise. Keep your mechs combat ready. This close to the heart of the Greenery, a counter attack against our offensive could come at any time."

Captain Merrick logged out of the comlink as suddenly as he had joined it, leaving the mech pilots no chance to ask questions or argue with him. No one tried to say anything anyway. The news of Colonel Jaeger coming to join them at the front was too inspiring, intimidating, and confusing all at once.

"Jaeger is one tough mother," Peter finally commented, breaking the silence.

"What?" Geddy asked as if he hadn't heard Peter clearly. Campbell doubted it was because of any technical issue with *Entropic Rush*'s systems. More than likely, Geddy was already fantasizing about what he and Lillian would be up to once the assault on the capital was finished.

"Peter said that Jaeger is one tough mother," Lillian answered. "When he was a mech pilot, Jaeger held the record for true kaiju kills until Peter took it from him with *Hulking Diablo*."

"Oh," Geddy commented, sounding totally uninterested.

"Steel Heart colonels don't usually lead from the front," Duvall pointed out.

"Hey," Dundee laughed. "If he's a good enough pilot to impress Peter, of all people, then we know the guy can fight. That's all that matters right?"

"You talk like he's going to be piloting a mech," Captain Mitch cut in. "I don't see how that's possible. Even if he got clearance from the Council of Engineers to bring one of the two that were left in Steel Heart to the front, he couldn't get it here in a reasonable amount of time. Captain Merrick made it sound like the colonel would be arriving in just a few hours or less."

"You don't think he's being flown in to take over one of ours do you?" Peter asked, sounding worried, an unusual thing for him. "I'll tell you right now he ain't getting *Hulking Diablo* except over my dead body."

"Calm it, Peter," Captain Mitch ordered. "Merrick didn't say anything about the colonel taking one of ours."

"Merrick didn't say much at all," Geddy sighed. "As much as I loathe to say it, I agree with Peter though. None of us should be ordered to give up our mechs at this late stage in the operation. We all know our mechs better than anyone else regardless of how good they used to be or are."

"I said drop it, Lieutenant Leigh, and I meant it," Captain Mitch snapped. "The colonel is the colonel so he can do whatever the devil he wants. I think we're all clear on that, aren't we?"

"Yes, sir," everyone chorused together, even Peter.

"Now keep your systems geared up and battle ready," Captain Mitch ordered. "If you see anything that could be a threat, take it out before it takes us out. We'll deal with everything else after the colonel arrives and we see what he has planned. Until then, let's just focus on doing our jobs, people."

****

Joster's interrogation by Major Rowley had been cut short. A second group of Tech forces, accompanied by three more of the giant mechs that were their primary weapons, arrived and the major had been called away to deal with more important matters Joster supposed. He had been left under the watch of two Tech infantry troopers for the last hour. With his fate still uncertain, each minute of waiting grew more painful than the one before it.

Finally, Major Rowley did return. He was accompanied by another man who introduced himself as Captain Merrick. Joster couldn't tell which one of them was in charge. Honestly, the two of them acted unsure on that fact themselves. Joster believed that a major outranked a captain but he couldn't recall for sure. Ranks in the Greenery were of an entirely different structure than what the Techs used.

"Your name is Joster, right?" Captain Merrick asked.

Joster nodded his head. "Yes, sir," he answered nervously, wondering why his name even mattered to the captain.

"Good." The captain smiled. "I like to know who I am speaking with, Joster. It makes things a bit more civil from my perspective. I understand that Steel Heart and your Greenery are at war but that doesn't mean we're not all humans."

Joster noticed Major Rowley raise an eyebrow. Apparently, Major Rowley didn't agree with the captain that folks from the Greenery were humans. Joster couldn't blame him. His time with Worm had enlightened him that maybe, just maybe, they weren't. Everyone in the Greenery underwent genetic manipulation to some extent or another before they were born and the higher classes underwent a lot more as they grew older. He knew some officers that were part animal in a sense, their eyes traded for those of cats, their muscles enhanced with those of apes, etc.

"Joster, we need you to tell us whatever you can about your capital's defenses," Captain Merrick urged him. "Us having that knowledge might save some lives on both sides when the fighting starts."

"I'm just a grunt," Joster admitted. "I drove a transport truck until one of your mechs blew my unit to bits."

"See?" Captain Merrick turned to Major Rowley. "Being polite and explaining your intent will get you a lot more information than pressure and fear tactics."

Major Rowley grunted. "Who says I wasn't being polite?"

Captain Merrick ignored him, returning his attention to Joster. "I understand that you weren't an officer, son, but surely you've been to the capital. Anything at all you can tell us is better than nothing."

"We don't have time for this," Major Rowley growled, drawing his sidearm. "The colonel is on his way here as we speak."

Major Rowley leveled the barrel of his pistol at Joster's head. "This is your last chance. Start talking now or ..."

"Major!" Captain Merrick snapped. "Put that gun away. Now."

"*Captain*," Rowley spat the word as a reminder of the other's rank. "We may share joint command of Battlegroup Alpha for the moment but don't forget that overall, I still outrank you."

Joster couldn't believe the two of them were having it out in front of him. Such arguments among officers were common in the Greenery but he had always figured that the Tech army ran much more professionally. The stories about it always implied that it did. Something clearly had Major Rowley shaken up and on edge and he was dang sure it wasn't him.

"Look," Joster broke into their argument. "I can't tell you anything about the capital and its defenses that you don't already know but I can tell you that. . ."

Major Rowley squeezed the trigger of his pistol before Joster could finish. Joster's eyes blinked in surprise as the barrel of the weapon flashed and he felt something smack into his forehead. The world turned black as his eyes stopped functioning. There was an intense sensation of falling and then nothing.

"What in the devil did you do that for?" Captain Merrick raged, staring in disbelief at where Joster's corpse lay sprawled out on the sand. Blood and brain matter oozed from the jagged exit wound on the backside of his skull where the major's bullet had blown through it.

"He was only wasting our time," Major Rowley snapped. "We have much more important things we should be dealing with and now we can."

"I'm going to report this," Captain Merrick growled at Major Rowley.

"Do what you like, Captain." Major Rowley shrugged, appearing unconcerned. "He said himself that he was just a grunt and of no use to us."

"That doesn't mean he didn't have rights," Captain Merrick protested. "He looked as human as either of us is, maybe more."

Major Rowley was already walking away back towards the makeshift command center of Battlegroup Alpha and paid no mind to his words at all.

"Bastard," Captain Merrick muttered under his breath. "If we live through this mess, you're going to pay for this, Major. Count on it."

Captain Merrick followed Major Rowley into the APC turned command center. It was nice to step inside its air-conditioned interior and out of the harsh sun that beat down on the sands of the Waste. Lieutenant Hawk, who sat the APC's comm. and sensors station, looked at them both as they entered as if unsure who to report to and then just started talking.

"Colonel Jaeger has reported that he is less than two hours away from arriving, sir," Lieutenant Hawk said. "He plans to take over full command of Battlegroup Alpha upon his arrival."

"Did he say anything about how he's getting here so quickly?" Major Rowley asked.

"Yes, sir, he did," Lieutenant Hawk answered. "Colonel Jaeger claims to be in route aboard a flight-capable mech that he is piloting."

Captain Merrick glanced over at Rowley to see the major appeared to be just as confused as he was.

"I didn't know such a thing existed," Major Rowley commented.

"Me either," Captain Merrick admitted. "Though, I am just a tanker and not a mech expert."

"The strange thing is …" Lieutenant Hawk added, "… that we also received a transmission from the Council of Engineers. Councilor James has ordered for Colonel Jaeger to be placed under immediate arrest for treason against Steel Heart upon the colonel's arrival."

"That makes even less sense," Captain Merrick grumbled.

"Actually, it explains a lot," Major Rowley disagreed. "It sounds like someone back home built an unregistered mech and the colonel has absconded with it."

"Colonel Jaeger would never do anything to betray Steel Heart," Captain Merrick said. "If someone did build a flight-capable mech and kept it a secret, then there was a bloody good reason the colonel took it rather than impounding it and bringing its creator in for treason."

"Regardless of the reason, treason is treason," Major Rowley countered.

"We're not arresting the colonel without more information about what's going on," Captain Merrick said and meant it.

"We'll do as we were ordered to do," Major Rowley moved to draw his sidearm but Captain Merrick stepped forward, catching the major's hand moving to the weapon by the wrist as he laid his arm flat against the major's throat, shoving the major into the APC's wall.

Major Rowley struggled against his hold but Captain Merrick held him tight, the pressure of his arm against the major's neck keeping him from saying anything more.

"I've had enough for your hotheadedness, Major," Captain Merrick warned Rowley. "Everyone of this command center's crew around us just saw you attempting to draw your weapon on a fellow officer. You are relieved of command until such time as the colonel deems fit to restore it to you."

Taking Major Rowley's weapon and aiming it at him, Captain Merrick backed away from the red-faced major.

"You there!" Captain Merrick yelled at the two guards outside of the makeshift command center's doors. "Take this man in custody and find somewhere safe to tuck him away until the colonel arrives."

"Yes, sir," the guards replied rushing to take hold of Major Rowley by his upper arms.

"You can't do this, Merrick!" Major Rowley spat. "I outrank you!"

"Not anymore," Captain Merrick said and was done with the matter.

The two guards hauled the still screaming major out of the APC and away from Captain Merrick's sight.

"Now then," Captain Merrick addressed Lieutenant Hawk. "Did the colonel say anything else?"

Lieutenant Hawk looked as if he wanted to crawl up under his console and hide there. Captain Merrick couldn't blame him for it. He had taken a big chance relieving Rowley of command, and if he was proven wrong in doing so, they would all pay for it.

"Yes, sir," Lieutenant Hawk answered reluctantly. "He said to start the attack on the Greenery's capital at once."

Captain Merrick locked the fingers of his hands together and stretched out his arms popping their joints. "Well then, we had best be about it ..."

****

Duala Mate Denkirch's lips parted in a feral snarl as he reached out with his mind and touched the minds of the Greenery's new batch of true kaiju. Power like he had never felt flowed through him. There were thirty-eight of the giant beasts. Denkirch had controlled true kaiju before but never so many and never from such a close proximity. The great beasts were fully grown and battle ready. Their growth acceleration had done its job perfectly.

The gates of the Greenery capital opened as Denkirch mentally urged the great beasts through them. The kaiju flyers tasked with reconnaissance of the Steel Heart forces near the capital had given him the exact location of those forces. It was confirmed that there were indeed seven mechs among their numbers. *Seven against thirty-eight,* Denkirch thought. *Indeed, the battle would be a short one.* The Steel Heart invaders would never suspect the Greenery to have such strength at its disposal in so short a time.

The lead kaiju was a beast out of legend. It stood a towering, three hundred feet tall. Its scales gleamed in the rays of the sun as it led the other kaiju out of the capital towards where the Steel Heart forces were preparing their assault. The ground shook with each step of its massive, clawed feet. The great beast's eyes glowed a hot red so bright they looked like mini-red suns within their sockets. Thickly muscled arms dangled at the great beast's sides as it tromped its way onward. Its claws flexed at the ends of those arms in eager anticipation of the battle it sensed awaited it.

As strong as he was, not even Duala Mate Denkirch could maintain control over so many true kaiju. He released the bulk of the monsters and focused his mental control solely on their fearsome leader. The other great beasts were content in following it anyway. Like the people of the Greenery, the kaiju they created deferred to power. The kaiju were far more intelligent than the mere animal-like monsters they appeared to be in some ways. They were cunning and acknowledged an alpha when they saw one. And there was no doubt that the three-hundred-foot monster leading their progression was the alpha of this batch of kaiju. They would follow it into battle without needing Denkirch's mental presence inside their minds to instruct them to do so. Battle and destruction were what came naturally to the monsters. It was encoded in their very DNA.

The journey was unexpectedly short. The Tech forces had apparently gotten moving since the last report from the flyers. They were approaching the city as Denkirch saw them through the lead Kaiju's eyes. A formation of smaller mechs led the battlegroup. Behind them came the Tech's hover tanks with the seven, giant mechs, who were the real threat, bringing up the rear. The Techs looked to have been expecting the Greenery to make its stand from behind the walls of the capital. They were utterly unprepared for the army of giant kaiju that they found themselves facing.

The formations of the smaller mechs and hover tanks broke up, veering away to the sides to take up firing positions as they moved out of the mechs' path. Denkirch smiled, causing the lead kaiju to bear its razor-like rows of teeth. Under his control, the massive, lead kaiju picked up its speed, charging directly at the seven mechs waiting ahead of it.

****

"All units break formation!" Captain Merrick yelled over the battlegroup's comlink as the army of kaiju came into view. His heart had skipped a beat as he saw the monsters. There were over three dozen of them, all the giant, true kaiju that were the Greenery's primary weapons. How the Greenery had shielded the kaiju from the battlegroup's sensors, he had no idea, nor did he have the time to try to figure it out. The Greenery was supposed to be stripped of resources and without any real number of the giant beasts to deploy against them. He had been expecting to fight his way through the capital's walls and carry the battle into its streets. Failing that, he had expected a siege of the Greenery's capital. Nothing had given any sign that the Greenery had such great beasts to bring against him and his men and certainly not in these kinds of numbers. He didn't allow himself to think about how many lesser kaiju had to be waiting in reserve if the battlegroup managed to survive against the giant kaiju and that was an unlikely proposition at best.

"Pick your targets and fire at will!" Captain Merrick ordered.

The hover tanks had spread out into a "V" formation, lining themselves up along what would surely be the sidelines of the main event between the great beasts and mechs under his command. They opened fire. Their main guns flashed as they hammered the fastest of the kaiju that were leading the charge toward the mechs. Bolts of pure energy tore at scale-covered kaiju flash as a barrage of shells accompanied them. The shells exploded on impact as they struck the faster of the kaiju. Captain Merrick didn't delude himself into thinking that his tanks were going to make much difference in this engagement. They had the firepower to hurt the kaiju but not to take them down, at least not easily.

The squad of Wolf-class mechs joined in, their hand-held rail-guns and machine guns chattering loudly as they fired a continuous stream of high-powered, armor-piercing rounds into the two kaiju directly behind the largest of the beasts. They concentrated their fire on the legs of the two kaiju, trying to take them down in the path of the others behind them.

The mechs split up into one group of three and two pairs of two, knowing that none of them would survive very long without another mech watching their back. *Four-Arm Fury, Entropic Rush,* and *Steadfast Warrior* held their ground against the center of the kaiju charge while the other two pairs of mechs separated, one to the right and one to the left, charging forward to keep the three of them from being immediately overwhelmed.

Four-Arm Fury engaged the largest of the kaiju which was leading the attack. She sprang forward, one of her four, clenched metal fists delivering a nasty upper-cut to the great beast that rattled its teeth and knocked it several steps backwards. Had the beast been human, Lillian would have almost sworn that it was grinning as it righted itself and reached out for *Four-Arm Fury.* She barely had time for *Four-Arm Fury* to dodge the swing the great beast took at her. Lillian could see she was going to be in for the fight of her life. *Four-Arm Fury*'s other main arm brought its fist around in mighty arc as it smashed into the side of the kaiju's jaw. This time, the kaiju stopped sneering at several of its razor-like teeth flew from its mouth in a splash of greenish-yellow blood. Lillian pressed *Four-Arm Fury*'s attack, lunging in to take a third swing at the great beast. The kaiju caught her fist in one of its massive, clawed hands before it made contact. *Four-Arm Fury*'s servos whined at max power as Lillian tried to free the mech's hand from the kaiju's grasp. Already sensing that her mech wasn't going to have the power to do that, she lurched *Four-Arm Fury* forward, closer to the great beast. *Four-Arm Fury*'s secondary arms moved like pistons, slamming their fists into the kaiju's lower body again and again. The great beast let out a roar of anger and twisted the arm of the mech that it still clutched. In a shower of sparks, *Four-Arm Fury*'s main right arm was pulled from its body. The kaiju flipped the arm over in its grasp and used it like a baseball bat against the mech. *Four-Arm Fury*'s head was knocked sideways on its shoulders by its own dismembered arm with a loud clang. The mech staggered, nearly losing its footing. Lillian lashed out with the mech main left arm, grabbing hold of the great beast's shoulder, continuing to hold

Four-Arm Fury close enough to the kaiju so that the pounding the monster was taking from the mech's lower arms continued.

"Get out of there!" Lillian heard Geddy shout at her over the comm. She didn't believe in backing down from a fight.

Geddy, in *Entropic Rush,* moved to her side. On her tactical display, she saw Geddy extend *Entropic Rush*'s arms over and around *Four-Arm Fury*'s shoulders. Twin sprays of flechettes exploded from *Entropic Rush*'s palms, slicing scales and meat from the great beast's chest. If it had been angry before, the kaiju was royally ticked off now. It shoved *Four-Arm Fury* away from it straight into *Entropic Rush.* The two mechs toppled to the ground. Spots of the softer metal of *Entropic Rush*'s hull crunched and buckled from *Four-Arm Fury*'s weight coming down upon it. The massive, three-hundred-foot-tall Kaiju would have ended them both then and there had it not been for Captain Mitch in *Steadfast Warrior.*

Steadfast Warrior hurled itself forward, coming between the great beast and the two mechs on the ground in front of it. The air itself seemed to bristle with energy as *Steadfast Warrior*'s sword blade slashed through it to strike at the monster towering over them. *Steadfast Warrior*'s blade cut a deep groove across the kaiju's chest, adding to the existing carnage already there from *Entropic Rush*'s barrage of flechette fire. For the first time since the battle had begun, the kaiju shrieked in real pain. Its eyes blazed brighter as it caught *Steadfast Warrior*'s blade as Captain Mitch pulled it back, trying to ready it for another swing. The kaiju's fist closed over the blade, snapping it in half. Greenish-yellow blood dripped from its clenched fist that held the upper half of the broken sword. *Steadfast Warrior* had no time to dodge as the great beast rammed the portion of the sword it clutched directly into the mech's head and through it. The kaiju gave the blade a twist as metal scraped against metal before *Steadfast Warrior*'s head exploded upon its shoulders in a shower of sparks and flame. Black smoke rolled upwards toward the heavens from the spot where *Steadfast Warrior*'s head had been. The kaiju wasn't done with the mech yet though. It brought up one of its three-toed feet in a kick to *Steadfast Warrior*'s chest that caved in the armor there and sent the mech's headless form careening backwards to thud to the ground on its back.

Lillian had gotten *Four-Arm Fury* on its feet and was settling the mech into a combat stance as the great beast turned its attention towards her again.

"Move! Move! Move!" Geddy was shouting at her over the com-link. She didn't understand what he wanted her to do. If he was wanting her to make a run for it, Geddy could go to hell. *Four-Arm Fury* braced itself as the great beast charged towards the mech. Lillian held the mech firmly in place, its stabilizers at max levels, as the kaiju crashed into *Four-Arm Fury*. She had caught the kaiju with *Four-Arm Fury*'s remaining three arms and pushed the mech to its limits as it used the great beast's own momentum against it. *Four-Arm Fury* accomplished the impossible, lifting the great beast up over its head in a flipping motion that sent it flying to crash into the ground behind where it stood. Even kaiju had to breathe and the air was knocked from the great beast's lungs by its impact. Lillian whirled *Four-Arm Fury*, about to take advantage of the situation, but she found that *Entropic Rush* already was. Geddy had brought his mech over to the great beast and leaped onto its wounded chest. Both of

Entropic Rush's palm flechette launchers were pressed directly against the great beast as they opened fire. The kaiju's body shook and spasmed as Geddy emptied everything *Entropic Rush* had left in them into the monster. Finally, it lay still, greenish-yellow blood pouring from its corpse to stain the earth beneath where it lay.

Lillian was in shock that they had actually managed to beat the creature, so much so that she didn't see the warning on *Four-Arm Fury*'s tactical display until it was too late. They might have taken out the largest of the kaiju but there were still dozens more of the monsters on the battlefield. One of them, a tentacled abomination, crashed into *Four-Arm Fury* from behind. Its tentacles curled over the mech's shoulders and waist, wrapping themselves so tightly and with such strength that they crushed entire sections of *Four-Arm Fury*'s armor inward. Alarms were blinking and giving shrills cries all around the mech's pilot compartment where Lillian sat. There were fires burning throughout the *Four-Arm Fury*'s interior. Lillian saw that *Four-Arm Fury*'s power systems had been damaged and were at only forty percent. *Entropic Rush* didn't appear to be faring much better. Two more kaiju had closed in on her and were engaging her as she struggled to get to her feet from where she still sat atop the corpse of the largest kaiju. One of those two kaiju had the head of a shark and the hands at the end of its two arms didn't resemble hands at all. They more closely resembled two blades made out of bone and chitin. The monster was relentlessly pounding *Entropic Rush* from where it stood over the mech. *Entropic Rush* rocked with each blow. The other of the two kaiju was one of the rare hair-covered beasts that was more mammal than reptile. The monster looked like a deformed, five-eyed ape. For the time being, it was holding back so that "Axe-hands" could do its work. Lillian knew Geddy and *Entropic Rush* couldn't withstand such a beating for too much longer.

Four-Arm Fury struggled against the tentacles wrapped around it as they continued to grow tighter about its waist and shoulder joints. Lillian knew that she had to act quickly or she was dead. Using half of *Four-Arm Fury*'s remaining power, she sent a surge of energy along the exterior of the mech's hull. The tentacled kaiju squealed in pain, jerking away from *Four-Arm Fury*. As it did, Lillian spun *Four-Arm Fury* around to grab its throat with the mech's remaining primary hand. *Four-Arm Fury*'s metal fingers sunk into the soft flesh of the monster's throat and tore it out with single, yanking motion. The tentacled kaiju's cries of pain were cut short in an explosion of gore as *Four-Arm Fury*'s hand came away from its throat with a fistful of flesh and other tissues. The tentacled kaiju dropped to its knees, eyes going wide in horror, then thudded face first onto the ground.

Entropic Rush had managed to shove "Axe-hands" away from it enough to rise to its feet. It stood facing the ape-like kaiju as Lillian watched Geddy bring one of the mech's sonic-based weapons to bear on the monster. The ape-like kaiju clutched its ears in response to the mech's attack but it wasn't enough to save it. Blood ran through its hairy fingers and along the lengths of its arms before its head popped like an overripe melon. Bone fragments and brain matter splattered outward from its exploding head to splash onto *Entropic Rush*'s armor.

"Take that, you mother!" Lillian heard Geddy shouting the second before "Axe-hands" avenged the ape. "Axe-hands" brought one of its feet smashing at angle onto the backside of *Entropic Rush*'s right knee, shattering the joint there. *Entropic Rush* collapsed in front of the monster as it swung both of its axe hands together on the mech's head. Lillian screamed as the two blades cut through to touch each other inside the ragged mass of metal that had been *Entropic Rush*'s head only a fraction of a second before.

"You bastard!" Lillian raged as she kicked *Four-Arm Fury* into gear, charging towards "Axe-hands." The kaiju turned its head to look at her in the moment before *Four-Arm Fury* plowed into it. The mech and kaiju went down together in a mass of wrestling limbs.

****

Peter in *Hulking Diablo* and Duvall in *Nuke Fist* were making a game of the mess that Battlegroup Alpha had found itself caught in. The two of them had broken to the right at first but had plowed their way back around into the center of the kaiju charge, placing themselves directly between the kaiju horde and the position where Captain Mitch, Lillian, and Geddy were making their stand.

"Come on, man!" Peter complained as Duvall took out another of the kaiju. "That crap isn't fair!"

Duvall was laughing as the corpse of the kaiju he had just blown a hole through thudded to the ground.

"Not my fault you went with melee weapons, bro!" Duvall mocked him as he targeted another kaiju. *Nuke Fist*'s right hand was glowing. Heat and coils of pure energy leaked from its clenched fist as it powered up again. A ping sounded in Duvall's ear as the fist reached it its max charge.

Hulking Diablo was doing the grunt work of keeping the bulk of the kaiju held off *Nuke Fist* as Duvall took out the creatures one blast at a time. Already, *Hulking Diablo* had beheaded a kaiju, gutted a second, and left a third without its arm. The giant red mech was swinging its twin axes as fast as it could, hacking at one beast then another. It was taking a great deal of damage too in the process for its efforts which angered Peter to no end as Duvall stood back in *Nuke Fist* adding to the number of kaiju corpses littering the ground *Hulking Diablo*. Peter was happy to be racking up the kills but knew that even a mech like *Hulking Diablo* could only hold out so long.

Peter flinched inside *Hulking Diablo*'s pilot compartment as a kaiju unexpectedly managed to dodge the axe he had swung at its skull. The beast's neck was like the body of a snake, its tiny, fanged head at the top of it as the neck writhed above its body. Peter cursed *Hulking Diablo*'s engineers for the missed swing as the snake-necked kaiju took advantage of the awkward moment and struck at him. Its mouth opened as its neck angled about to bring the creature's head downward in a movement so fast the motion seemed to blur. The snake-like kaiju's fangs dug deep through the armor of *Hulking Diablo*'s left arm.

"Holy …" Peter wailed as he saw that the thing's fangs had injected the arm with something akin to acid. Metal burned and metal inside *Hulking Diablo*'s left arm as the servos there died and black smoke leaked out of the arm's joints. "You're going to pay for that!" Peter swore to the snake-like kaiju as *Hulking Diablo*'s left arm froze up completely and dangled limply at the mech's side. The axe clutched in the mech's left hand slid from its now limp fingers. The weapon bounced onto the ground at

Hulking Diablo's feet, nearly tripping it up as the mech backpedaled so that Peter could get another swing at the kaiju's writhing neck. This time, the blade of his right-handed axe struck it dead on, severing it. The kaiju's tiny head and a good-sized portion of its upper neck went flying away from the beast's body in a spray of rancid, black blood.

Two kaiju had moved around *Hulking Diablo* during its fight with the snake kaiju and were closing on *Nuke Fist*. Duvall saw them coming. The mech's fist was powered up again so he let the faster of the two have it. A sphere of energy formed around the fist, almost a third the size of the mech itself, and shot outward at the kaiju Duvall had targeted. It hit the kaiju in the center of its torso, vaporizing most of it. What was left of the kaiju collapsed in on itself and toppled to the ground, a smoking mass of burnt meat. Duvall already had the fist recharging as the other kaiju reached *Nuke Fist*. It was still two ticks away from being able to be fired again though. In order to buy time, Duvall brought *Nuke Fist*'s other arm up as a shield to block the blow of the kaiju's clawed hand. This kaiju was "old style" and very reptilian humanoid in its appearance and form. The kaiju's claws raked against the armor of *Nuke Fist*'s arm, but thankfully, the beast wasn't strong enough to get any real penetration with them. Their impact did force *Nuke Fist* to stagger though, which allowed the kaiju to take a second swing at its head. Duvall grunted as the claws slammed into the side of *Nuke Fist*'s head and he was jarred about inside the pilot compartment there. *Nuke Fist*'s system pinged to let Duvall know that the mech's primary weapon was charged again. Duvall brought the mech's glowing fist in to touch the scales of the kaiju's stomach as he fired the weapon. The energy from the mech's fist blast splattered bits of the kaiju everywhere as the point-blank shot ripped the monster apart in an explosion of cooked internals and bits that were scorched beyond identification. Duvall was about to give a victory cry when he heard Peter yelling, "Look out!"

The last thing Duvall ever saw was a geyser of fire that shot forth from the impossibly wide, open mouth of the dragon-faced kaiju he turned to face. The beast had flanked him and caught him utterly by surprise.

Peter watched as the fire breath of the dragon-faced kaiju melted away *Nuke Fist*'s head, right shoulder, and a good chunk of its upper right side. Streams of molten metal ran down over the curves of *Nuke Fist*'s legs as the dragon-faced kaiju continued to hose the mech with its breath.

Hulking Diablo's axe flew straight and true, spinning end over end through the air as the mech threw it at the dragon-faced kaiju. With a thunderous thunking noise, the axe embedded itself in the center of the dragon kaiju's forehead, splitting the top of the kaiju's dragon-like snout in the process. The dragon kaiju reeled about for a moment and then toppled over to lay dead near *Nuke Fist*'s molten remains.

There would be no retrieving of the weapon in the immediate future. Three more kaiju had come forward to engage *Hulking Diablo.* The red mech bent over and swept up the axe that had fallen from the hand of its disabled arm. A kaiju with the head of a toad and human-like arms rushed towards *Hulking Diablo* as the mech rose back up with the axe in hand. *Hulking Diablo* swung the axe as it rose, smashing the weapon into the lower portion of the toad-headed kaiju's face. The blade cut through flesh and bone alike, severing the toad kaiju's lower jaw in half. Spitting blood and pieces of the long tongue that had been curled up inside its mouth, the toad kaiju retreated, clearing the path for the monster behind it. The kaiju that sprang forward as it moved aside looked like a giant rat. It moved on all fours, its teeth snapping as the creature tried to bite away part of *Hulking Diablo*'s right leg. Peter wasn't having it though. *Hulking Diablo*'s axe blade came down the topside of the rat's neck. The blow didn't have the force to sever the rat's neck completely but it did cut through rat kaiju's spine. The rat kaiju flopped onto the ground, its legs giving way beneath it as it lost the ability to move anything below the spot where *Hulking Diablo* had hacked through its spine.

Ignoring the rat kaiju, with no time to finish it, *Hulking Diablo* yanked its remaining axe from the rat kaiju as a kaiju with horns covering the entirety of the top of its head roared. The monster lowered its head like a charging ram as it came, full out, at *Hulking Diablo*. Peter managed to dodge the attack, pushing the giant red mech to its limits, sidestepping it. The horned monster sped past *Hulking Diablo*. Keeping *Hulking Diablo*'s systems pushed beyond the red line, Peter poured on even more speed as the giant red mech whirled about in time to strike a blow with its axe before the monster was completely out of range. *Hulking Diablo*'s axe thudded into the meat and scales of the horned kaiju's side with the mech's arm extended to its max length. The kaiju howled in pain, the blade sliding free of its body, unable to bring itself to a halt.

Peter didn't even have time to curse as he brought the giant red mech around and saw still two more kaiju moving to engage *Hulking Diablo.*

****

Campbell, in *Ragnarok Valkyrie,* and Dundee, in *Boomerang Charge,* were holding their own against the pack of kaiju that they were engaged with. *Boomerang Charge*'s right arm was covered from wrist to shoulder with long, razor-like spikes which the mech used to tear the kaiju apart when it charged them. So far, the mech hadn't actually charged anything, but spikes were already dripping with blood from various kaiju that had made the mistake of trying to charge it. Dundee had been using the mech's spiked arm as a shield and bludgeoning weapon to great effect. When the chance presented itself, *Boomerang Charge* also hurled giant, razored boomerangs into the ranks of the kaiju. One kaiju had lost an arm to one of the weapons and another kaiju had the rear of a boomerang protruding from its chest where the weapon had sunk into the side of its ribcage. Streams of bubbling pink gore ran from the wound along the curves of the monster's body and down its legs.

The left arm of *Boomerang Charge* bore five of the boomerangs at the beginning of the battle. Now, the mech only had two left at its disposal, and with the kaiju's having surrounded them at close range, it was unlikely that were going to be any further use.

Thankful that the repair crew had been able to reattach and reload *Ragnarok Valkyrie*'s wrist cannons, Campbell made good use of the weapons. *Ragnarok Valkyrie* bobbed and weaved like a boxer as the kaiju around it took swings at its body. The mech managed to avoid the bulk of the blows as its wrist cannons blazed away at the beasts at point-blank range.

The two mechs had wounded a great deal more of the kaiju than they had actually been able to kill. They had been fighting a defensive battle and primarily trying to just hold the kaiju back from the other mechs up until now. With so many of their friends dead despite their efforts, Campbell figured it was time to change things up. He activated the switch that caused the charges that disengaged *Ragnarok Valkyrie*'s wrist-mounted cannons to be blown from where they were attached so that he could sling out the long, chain-mace weapons underneath them. The chain of the right mace extended, spilling out of the mech's arm so that its spiked head swept around in an arc to smash into the skull of a kaiju with glowing blue eyes. Bone caved inward as blood splashed from where the head of the mace made contact. A hair-covered, bipedal, dog kaiju hurried towards *Ragnarok Valkyrie,* snarling as it came. Campbell lashed out with the mech's other chain mace. Its chain wrapped around the dog kaiju's lower left leg, and with a mighty yank, *Ragnarok Valkyrie* jerked the dog kaiju off its feet. Before the monster could recover, Campbell slammed one of the mech's massive, metal feet downward onto the center of the dog kaiju's chest. The foot went through the monster's body in an explosion of blood, shattering its ribcage in the process.

"We can't hold these things much longer, Campbell," Dundee yelled at him over the comm.

"We don't need to hold them anymore," Campbell spat back. "We just need to kill them all before they kill us!"

"Right," Dundee shouted. "I hear ya, mate. I think I'm gonna bloody well give that a shot. You better stay the hell out of my way."

Campbell watched *Boomerang Charge* bash a kaiju away from it with its spiked arm and start running towards the center of the pack of kaiju in front of them. He realized at once what Dundee was up to.

"Don't do it, man!" Campbell screamed helplessly. "It's not worth it!"

If Dundee heard him though, the actions of *Boomerang Charge* gave no sign of it. The yellow-streaked mech built up speed as it raced towards the kaiju. Its spiked arm was braced and ready to plow into them, but Campbell knew that didn't matter if he was right about what Dundee had planned.

"All remaining units," Dundee cried on the comm. "Take cover if you can!"

Ragnarok Valkyrie's armored hands snatched up the body of the dog kaiju it had just killed and held the corpse up as a shield in the direction of *Boomerang Charge* just as the mech rammed into the mass of the kaiju. *Boomerang Charge* self-destructed in a blast that shook the entire field of battle. The mech and seven kaiju vanished in the flash of a fusion-powered explosion that was so bright, it nearly blinded Campbell despite *Ragnarok Valkyrie*'s protection systems and the mech turning its head away from the blast.

It was enough to bring a halt to the battle. The surviving kaiju pulled back to regroup as the remaining mechs did the same.

****

Hulking Diablo, one arm dangling at its side and its body marked terribly by kaiju claws and teeth, stumbled over to stand at *Ragnarok Valkyrie*'s right side. *Four-Arm Fury* limped up to take a position to *Ragnarok Valkyrie*'s left. The mech didn't have four arms anymore. One of its two primary ones had been broken off at its elbow joint and its two lower arms were gone entirely. Sparking wires and circuitry spilled out from jagged tears along over *Four-Arm Fury*'s torso. Campbell was shocked to see that the three of them were all that as left and equally as shocked that Lillian's mech was even still standing given the apparent amount of damage it had suffered.

Battlegroup Alpha's hover tanks had only taken minimum losses and Captain Merrick had them form up to the rear of the group of mechs. Of the six, smaller Wolf-class mechs, there was no sign. Campbell presumed they had been lost as well.

"That did *not* go as planned," Peter growled over the comm.

Of the thirty-eight, true kaiju, sixteen of the monsters remained. A few of the creatures were wounded but their snarls, roars, and hisses left no doubt that they were all still in the fight.

"What do we do now?" Campbell heard himself ask.

"Saying a prayer wouldn't be a bad idea," Captain Merrick answered.

"Screw that," Lillian raged. "Let's kill the rest of those fraggers and be done with this."

"What in the devil did they all come from anyway?" Peter asked. "I thought this place was supposed to be empty of those things. I mean, isn't that why we're here? To take advantage of how weak they were supposed to be?"

"The rumors were true," Captain Merrick said, his voice strangely calm given what they faced. "The Greenery has found a means to mass produce kaiju like nothing we've ever seen before. We all need to hope that these are the only ones they have ready or we're dead no matter what we do."

"I'd say we're dead anyway," Peter snorted.

A noise from somewhere above and to the north of the field of battle turned the heads of the mechs and the kaiju alike skyward. A mech with giant straight wings stretching out from the sides of its body came streaking through the clouds like a guided rocket. It slowed at the last instant as it brought its legs forward to land on them directly in front of *Ragnarok Valkyrie, Hulking Diablo,* and *Four-Arm Fury*. Once on the ground, it drew a giant-sized, glowing broadsword from a sheath positioned between the engines on its back.

Peter whistled in appreciation of how smoothly and human-like the flying mech moved.

"This is Colonel Jaeger piloting Samurai One," the colonel's voice boomed over Battlegroup Alpha's comlink. "Captain Merrick, you are relieved of command. I'll be taking over things from here on in."

"I stand relieved, sir," Captain Merrick answered happily. "Glad to have you with us, sir."

"That mech can't be legal," someone, likely in one of the captain's tanks, muttered over the comm.

"Belay that kind of talk, soldier!" Campbell heard Colonel Jaeger snap. "All that matters right now is that we live through this fight and that city over there is burnt to ashes."

"Sir," Captain Merrick spoke up.

"What is it, Captain?" Colonel Jaeger asked, sounding as if his patience had already been stretched to its limit.

"Something is happening with the kaiju, sir," Captain Merrick informed him.

Campbell tore his attention away from the gleaming mech that Colonel Jaeger was piloting. He looked over at where the kaiju were licking their wounds and getting ready to charge at them again to see over half the monsters simply melting away where they stood. Flesh liquefied and flowed from their bones. The unaffected kaiju were mewling and backing away from their dying brethren in abject horror.

"What the hell?" Campbell heard Colonel Jaeger exclaim.

****

Duala Mate Denkirch's mind had been nearly torn asunder as the largest of the kaiju had died. His mind had been one with the creature's in that moment. The psychic backlash was so intense that he lay, sprawled out on the floor with blood leaking from the corners of his eyes, mouth, nose, and ears. Denkirch's sanity had always been questionable at the best of times. Now, he was stark-raving mad and Grand Duala Minerva saw that in his eyes as he painfully got to his feet. She realized with a start that the psychic backlash wasn't all that was wrong with him and turned her gaze away from him.

"What have you done, Denkirch?" she rasped as he gave her a crooked smile.

"I've done what you never dared to do, Minerva," he spoke softly, his voice almost a whisper. "I have performed the rite of transference."

"You're insane," Grand Duala Minerva stammered, retreating from him.

"Am I?" Denkirch shrugged. "Look at me!" he yelled.

Grand Duala Minerva didn't need to look at him to sense that he had drunk the power of several of the true kaiju into himself. He had stolen their lives and taken their power through the rite of transference. The rite was ancient and only she was supposed to know how to perform it. Somehow, Denkirch must have touched her own mind at some point and raped it for the knowledge that came with the title of Grand Duala.

"I said look at me!" Denkirch hissed. The very walls of the chambers shook and cracked from the power of his voice.

Slowly, she turned her gaze upon him once more. Denkirch's body bristled with pure, unadulterated power. He had grown to twice the size he had been, now standing over fourteen feet tall. The top of his head brushed the high ceiling of the room as he moved about.

"You've destroyed us all, Denkirch," she spat at him. "You can't possibly control all that power. It will drive you mad."

Denkirch laughed. It was a loud and horrid sound like nails running across the surface of an Old World blackboard. "What does that matter? According to you, I am mad already."

"Stop this now and release what you have taken," she ordered him, finding the courage to stand in his path as he started for the window of the chamber that looked out over the walls of the city to the battlefield beyond it.

"I think not." Denkirch grinned. "Not until Steel Heart is broken and we of the Greenery rule supreme once and for all."

Summoning up all the power that resided in her as Grand Duala, Minerva shoved her hands forward in front of her body as arcs of crackling, burning energy leaped from her fingers at Denkirch. They struck him without any real effect.

Denkirch looked down at his chest where the bolts had struck him and then back at her as the grin he wore grew wider.

"That was a mistake, Minerva," he cackled wildly. "I was going to let you live if no other reason than the amusement of doing so. Now, however …"

Denkirch's jaw disjointed, extending impossibly wide, as a geyser of vomit-like fluid burst from it to splash over her where she stood. The bile burned away her flesh and dissolved her bones, leaving nothing more of her than a pool of bubbling liquid upon the floor in her place.

As his jaw snapped back into place, Denkirch ran towards the chamber's window facing the battlefield and jumped through it. He took flight, the strength of his telekinesis propelling through the air.

****

Colonel Jaeger stared at the ten puddles of gore and liquefied meat that had moments before been giant kaiju. He didn't have a clue what had happened to the monsters or what was keeping the remaining six from moving forward to attack *Samurai One* and the other mechs.

Movement in the air drew his attention. Something small but far too large to be a man despite its shape came flying out of the Greenery capital, over its walls, to land in front of the remaining kaiju. Whatever it was, it was registering at a power level that dwarfed even *Samurai One*'s.

"I am Grand Duala Denkirch," an inhuman voice hissed inside Colonel Jaeger's head. He knew all too well that the soldiers and citizens of the Greenery possessed varying degrees of psionic abilities, but in all his years, he had never had one of them address him telepathically like this.

Colonel Jaeger had no doubt that the telepathic voice was coming from the nearly fifteen-foot-tall man who stood among the six kaiju that had survived whatever had turned the others into piles of goo. The six kaiju had stood up to their full heights as the man landed among them as if they were acknowledging the man as their leader.

Flipping on the external megaphones of *Samurai One,* Colonel Jaeger responded, "Well, Grand Duala Denkirch, did you come out to make your surrender on behalf of the Greenery personally?"

Denkirch's laughter echoed inside Jaeger's mind.

"Hardly," Denkirch growled. "I've come to end this."

As Lillian screamed a rage-filled battle cry, *Four-Arm Fury* lumbered forward at the best speed the badly damaged mech could muster. The man, Denkirch, made no move to flee from *Four-Arm Fury*'s path or did the six kaiju move to stop it. Instead, Denkirch merely raised a hand in the mech's direction. Shimmering tentacles of telekinetic power lashed out from his hand to strike at the mech. One wrapped around the mech's last remaining arm, snapping it from its body. Another sunk into the guts of the mech like a spear, a large section of the *Four-Arm Fury*'s back exploded in a blossoming exit wound of flames and debris as it passed through the mech's body. A third tentacle finished what the second had started and cleaved the entire mech in two. *Four-Arm Fury*'s top half slid away from its bottom as both halves fell in different directions to thud upon the ground.

"Lillian!" Campbell heard Peter howl over the comm. He knew Peter respected Lillian a great deal, though he would hardly call the two of them friends. Peter didn't really have friends, only colleagues and enemies.

"I'm okay," Lillian's pained voice spoke up over the comm. "Kill that bastard for me."

"Consider it done," Peter laughed. *Hulking Diablo*'s good arm drew back and flung the mech's last axe at … whatever the Hades Denkirch was. An invisible force of some kind caught the spinning axe halfway to him and flung it back at the giant red mech. *Hulking Diablo* had no time to attempt to dodge the unexpected counterattack. Its own sword sliced into its chest and *Hulking Diablo*'s upper body exploded in a blast that shook Campbell where he sat in *Ragnarok Valkyrie*'s pilot compartment.

"All units," Colonel Jaeger shouted, "engage that bastard and take him out! I'll handle the kaiju!"

Samurai One moved so fast it seemed to blur as it waded into the ranks of the remaining kaiju. Its blade claimed the head of one in a shower of steaming black blood. Spinning its sword around, *Samurai One* impaled another before the great beasts were even able to start moving. One of the kaiju, a truly reptilian creature, raked at the mech with its claws. The kaiju's claws broke as they met the metal of *Samurai One*'s armor. The great beast squealed in pain for a fraction of a second before the blade of *Samurai One*'s sword split its skull in half along the middle of its head. Already yanking the blade free of the great beast's mangled head, *Samurai One* spun about as the last three kaiju charged it at once. Colonel Jaeger managed to punch the fastest of the kaiju in the face with *Samurai One*'s clenched left fist. The great beast stumbled backwards, spitting blood and teeth as the engines on the mech's back spat flames and launched *Samurai One* upwards into the sky. The kaiju leaking blood from its lips, flattened nose, and the dent inward middle of its forehead collapsed to thrash about in its death throes. The other two kaiju charged through the spot where it had been, ramming into one another. One of the beasts fell to smash its snout into the ground but the other jerked about making a grab for the mech's leg. The clawed fingers of its right hand closed around *Samurai One*'s left ankle. With all its strength, the kaiju roared, emptying its massive lungs of air as it yanked the flying mech from the air and smashed it down to land on its side. *Samurai One*'s sword was knocked from the mech's grasp and went bouncing away from it. The kaiju hurled itself on top of the mech before Colonel Jaeger could get it back on its feet. The impact rocked the colonel in *Samurai One*'s pilot compartment so fiercely that the motion broke the colonel's neck. The lights of *Samurai One*'s eyes flickered out as her pilot died. She slumped beneath the raging kaiju on top of her.

Campbell was there though. He had brought *Ragnarok Valkyrie* up behind the kaiju and took its head with both of the giant mech's hand. With a sharp twist and the whine of servo motors, *Ragnarok Valkyrie* ripped the monster's head from its shoulders.

Captain Merrick's command tank and the other hover tanks had engaged the thing that was Denkirch. Their main guns were emptying their magazines of shells at the man. None of the shells were reaching their target though. Denkirch had flung up some kind of mental shield that stopped them before reached him. They exploded, lethal fireworks flashing red, yellow, and orange against the invisible barrier he had created.

Denkirch retaliated with a pulse of telekinetic energy that blew three of the tanks apart with a single swipe of his hand.

"Campbell!" Captain Merrick shouted over the battlegroup's shared comlink.

He hoped that Captain Merrick and his tankers could hold on because *Ragnarok Valkyrie* found herself locked in combat with the last two of the great kaiju. Releasing one of the mech's long, chain maces again, Campbell slashed one through the air at the side of the closest kaiju's head. The beast avoided the mace's head only to have its chain wrap around its neck like a bola. Using the chain to drag the beast to it, *Ragnarok Valkyrie* took hold of the chain with both hands and used it strangle the beast to death.

Campbell wondered why the last of the kaiju hadn't attacked during his struggle with the creature he had just choked to death. He scanned *Ragnarok Valkyrie*'s tactical display for the beast's location to see that the kaiju was dead. One of the hover tanks had scored a lucky shot on it. The great beast's corpse lay on the ground, black tendrils of smoke rising from the mangled remnants its right eye socket.

"Campbell!" Captain Merrick cried again over the comm.

Ragnarok Valkyrie turned towards where the hover tanks were going head to head Denkirch. Only Captain Merrick's command tank and two others were still in the battle. The rest were destroyed. Their burnt-out and crushed hulls littered the battlefield. As Campbell watched, the three tanks fired in unison at Denkirch. Their shells detonated short of their target, striking a nearly invisible shield composed of psychic energy. Campbell knew he had to take Denkirch out. The question was how. The man had just slaughtered almost all of Battlegroup Alpha's tanks by himself. He had to try though. If he didn't, Captain Merrick and the others were dead. *Ragnarok Valkyrie* slung one of its chain maces over its head, building up speed and power with the weapon. The head of the mace swung downward in a mighty arc at the fifteen-foot-tall, glowing man named Denkirch. The mace hit Denkirch's protective shield with enough force to shatter the skull of a kaiju. The shockwave of the impact rocked the nearby tanks. Denkirch's shield held if only barely. The man dropped to his knees, weakened, his glowing eyes turning to look upwards at *Ragnarok Valkyrie*.

Campbell cursed as Denkirch raised a hand towards *Ragnarok Valkyrie*. Energy bolts rippled outward from the man's fingertips. They tore *Ragnarok Valkyrie*'s right leg. Jagged bits of half melted armor flew from where the energy bolts. Cursing, Campbell set into action a desperate plan.

"Captain Merrick!" Campbell yelled. "Get your tanks out of here."

Campbell watched as the tanks started moving, speeding away from Denkirch and the Greenery's capital. The attack on Denkirch's shield and the bolts he had fired that ripped up *Ragnarok Valkyrie*'s right leg below the knee appeared to take a lot out of him. Campbell gave Captain Merrick a moment to get his tanks clear as Denkirch took a moment to recover.

Keying in the code that sent *Ragnarok Valkyrie*'s reactor into a critical overload, Campbell did his best to make peace with God. If his plan worked, neither he nor Denkirch was going to live longer than another few seconds.

Ragnarok Valkyrie flung herself at Denkirch like a soldier leaping onto a grenade to save his friends only *Ragnarok Valkyrie* was the grenade. Campbell died instantly as the mech landed on top of Denkirch and her reactor blew in a blast as hot, bright, and powerful as a small-scale nuclear detonation.

****

"Frag me!" Captain Merrick cried out as the giant mech exploded several miles behind his fleeing command tank. Its driver had been pushing the heavy vehicle's fans to their limit in an attempt to get away from the battle between the mech and the mutated man who seemed to have the power of a demi-god. The shockwave of the blast jarred Captain Merrick forward in his command seat. The command tank's systems flickered, threatening to shut down, and then crackled back to life.

Alpha Tango 23 died in the shockwave but Alpha Tango 16 continued to match the speed of Captain Merrick's own tank. The two hover tanks kept moving at max speed on a course that took them out of Greenery territory.

Captain Merrick counted himself lucky to be alive. There were no giant kaiju left to pursue his command tank and Alpha Tango 16. After reaching what he felt was a safe distance, Captain Merrick calmed enough to dispatch a recon drone. It streaked across the sky back towards the Greenery capital.

The data streaming in from the drone confirmed that both *Ragnarok Valkyrie* and the man named Denkirch were no more.

The walls of the Greenery's capital were scorched and caved in at several places along their length, but the city itself behind them was largely untouched by the explosion generated by the mech's overloading reactor except for the buildings along its northern edge. That had struck a powerful blow against the Greenery but Captain Merrick knew it wasn't enough.

"It was all in vain," Captain Merrick muttered, shaking his head.

"What's that, sir?" the driver of his command tank asked.

"Nothing," Captain Merrick lied, attempting to mask the utter defeat he was feeling. "Just get us home as quickly as you can."

"Yes, sir!" his driver answered eagerly.

Captain Merrick removed his helmet and ran a finger through his sweat-slicked hair. The war between the Greenery and Steel Heart, it seemed, was far from over.

END

Eric S Brown is the author of numerous book series including the Bigfoot War series, the Kaiju Apocalypse series (with Jason Cordova), the Crypto-Squad series (with Jason Brannon), the Homeworld series (With Tony Faville and Jason Cordova), the Jack Bunny Bam series, and the A Pack of Wolves series. Some of his stand alone books include War of the Worlds plus Blood Guts and Zombies, World War of the Dead, Last Stand in a Dead Land, Sasquatch Lake, Kaiju Armageddon, Megalodon, Megalodon Apocalypse, Kraken, Alien Battalion, The Last Fleet, and From the Snow They Came to name only a few. His short fiction has been published hundreds of times in the small press in beyond including markets like the Onward Drake and Black Tide Rising anthologies from Baen Books, the Grantville Gazette, the SNAFU Military horror anthology series, and Walmart World magazine. He has done the novelizations for such films as Boggy Creek: The Legend is True (Studio 3 Entertainment) and The Bloody Rage of Bigfoot (Great Lake films). The first book of his Bigfoot War series was adapted into a feature film by Origin Releasing in 2014. Werewolf Massacre at Hell's Gate was the second of his books to be adapted into film in 2015. Major Japanese publisher, Takeshobo, recently bought the reprint rights to his Kaiju Apocalypse series (with Jason Cordova) and it is slated for 2018 release in Japan. Ring of Fire Press will be releasing a collected edition of his Monster Society stories (set in the New York Times Best-selling world of Eric Flint's 1632) later this year. In addition to his fiction, Eric also writes an award winning comic book news column entitled "Comics in a Flash." Eric lives in North Carolina with his wife and two children where he continues to write tales of the hungry dead, blazing guns, and the things that lurk in the woods.

CHECK OUT OTHER GREAT KAIJU NOVELS

ATOMIC REX: WRATH OF THE POLAR YETI
by Matthew Dennion

It has been fifteen years since Captain Chris Myers used his giant mech to draw the kaiju of North America into each other's territory to have them destroy each other. Once all of the kaiju had battled to the death only Atomic Rex was left standing. In Antarctica, the kaiju known as Armorsaur has entered the frozen valley of the yetis and attacked them. Devouring all but one alpha male yeti who was exposed to the kaiju's blood and left dying in the snow. The yeti awoke to find himself transformed into a kaiju with an obsession to destroy Armorsaur. Chris and Kate are forced to protect the people of their settlement by drawing Atomic Rex into South America where he will battle the kaiju there to usurp their territory and claim their hunting grounds as his own. As Atomic Rex enters South America from the north the enraged Polar Yeti enters the continent from the south. The two most powerful kaiju in the world will battle their way through a multitude of giant monsters as they are set on a collision course with each other!

KAIJU CORPS
by Matthew Dennion

They are four soldiers who were genetically created to be mankind's last line of defense against potential world ending threats. They are soldiers who can transform themselves into gigantic monsters. They are the Kaiju Corps and they are facing a threat that is beyond the scope of even their fantastic abilities.

CHECK OUT OTHER GREAT KAIJU NOVELS

POLAR YETI AND THE BEASTS OF PREHISTORY
by Matthew Dennion

A team from Princeton University searching for a lost tribe in Antartica discover a hidden valley filled with wooly mammoths, saber toothed tigers and other Ice Age beasts. Seizing the opportunity of a lifetime, the team set up camp to study the amazing creatures. But there is something else that lives in the Valley. Something terrifying. Something beyond imagination. POLAR YETI!

TITAN WARS
by M.C. Norris

Millions of microscopic alien life forms escape a sample canister of water from the frigid depths of outer space. Invisible to the naked eye, a menacing menagerie of more than seventy deadly species react to Earth's warm and fertile seas by launching into metabolic overdrive. Waves of gargantuan abominations begin to rise from the sea, transforming our world into a zoo without cages, where humans plunge to the bottom of the food chain.

In dire need of a zookeeper, the Allied Navy turns to "Psyjack," a bickering geek squad with an outrageous plan to hack into the minds of the megafauna with some reengineered neurosurgical technology. The young gamers hope to level the uneven playing field by fighting monsters with monsters, but they couldn't have anticipated how deadly their technology could be, if it ever fell into the wrong hands ...

CHECK OUT OTHER GREAT KAIJU NOVELS

MURDER WORLD | KAIJU DAWN
by Jason Cordova
& Eric S Brown

Captain Vincente Huerta and the crew of the Fancy have been hired to retrieve a valuable item from a downed research vessel at the edge of the enemy's space.
It was going to be an easy payday.
But what Captain Huerta and the men, women and alien under his command didn't know was that they were being sent to the most dangerous planet in the galaxy.
Something large, ancient and most assuredly evil resides on the planet of Gorgon IV. Something so terrifying that man could barely fathom it with his puny mind. Captain Huerta must use every trick in the book, and possibly write an entirely new one, if he wants to escape Murder World.

KAIJU ARMAGEDDON
by Eric S. Brown

The attacks began without warning. Civilian and Military vessels alike simply vanished upon the waves. Crypto-zoologist Jerry Bryson found himself swept up into the chaos as the world discovered that the legendary beasts known as Kaiju are very real. Armies of the great beasts arose from the oceans and burrowed their way free of the Earth to declare war upon mankind. Now Dr. Bryson may be the human race's last hope in stopping the Kaiju from bringing civilization to its knees.
This is not some far distant future. This is not some alien world. This is the Earth, here and now, as we know it today, faced with the greatest threat its ever known. The Kaiju Armageddon has begun.